BY MADISON
ROSIPAL

MADISON ROSIPAL

My Mom The Intergalactic Terrorist

First edition

This book was professionally typeset on Reedsy.
Find out more at reedsy.com

Contents

Acknowledgement

I'd like to thank everyone who has stood by me as a writer. I never thought in a million years that I would ever be able to write let alone publish a book, but here we are. For everyone who has stood by me, my parents, my teachers, my friends, my family, and anyone who's ever humored me by reading something I wrote I give my greatest thanks.

For all of you who bought this book, thank you for supporting my dream.

1

Chapter 1

F rom its place in my pocket, my phone began to buzz, filling the air with the silly ringtone I'd chosen for my mother; the X-files theme, I thought it would go well with the cartoonish alien I'd selected for her contact image. With a sigh, I pulled it out and mashed the answer button in frustration.

"Galileo," my mother's voice came.

"What?" I asked.

"What do you want to smell like this week?"

That was her way of asking what scent of body wash I wanted. For some reason, she's convinced that people bathe to make them smell like something else and they put a lot of importance on said smell.

"Do they have anything like nature-ish? Any waterfall or stream?" I asked.

She went silent on the other end, but I could still hear the background noise of the grocery store, so I knew she didn't hang up. I could hear her grab a bottle on the other end, making a thoughtful noise as she looked it over.

"How about Ocean Breeze?"

"That works."

"Wonderful! And what would you like your hair to smell like?"

Groaning, I rolled my eyes, pinching the space between my brows. As I stepped, my foot connected with a loose stone, sending it skidding ahead of me on the sidewalk. I kicked it once again when I caught up to it but after that it was out of my sight.

"Just get me something clear. It doesn't matter the smell."

"Alright, but don't get mad at me if I pick something you don't like."

She takes this all too seriously.

"You don't have to call me every time you go grocery shopping mom."

"But I do! I want to make sure I get the right stuff," She complained.

"Whatever, I'll see you at home."

"Ok son, beep."

She thinks you're supposed to say beep when you turn the phone off. I think it's because she heard the phone beep and thought it was another person. Whatever, I wish she'd go back to whatever planet she came from, and return me to whatever family she abducted me from.

Before I could put my phone away, it buzzed again, this time it played the text notification sound that I had set for my buddy Nikki; Area 51, an excellent match to the history channel "Aliens" meme, the one with the guy with funny hair, that I had chosen for her photo.

"Earth to space cadet. Come in space cadet," the message read.

"This is space cadet. What's the problem?"

Nikki insists on calling me space cadet, that or Stargazer.

"Food supply running low. Requesting backup." Translation: "My parents are out of town again, and I don't want to cook for myself, so can I come over and bum a meal off you guys?"

"Of course."

Mom may be the strangest person in town, but she's never been one to turn down a hungry child. I could already smell what she was cooking when I walked into the house. It smelled like spaghetti, one of the things she's actually good at cooking. That's not saying much though, all you have to do is boil water and make sure you don't overcook the noodles.

The big pot on the stove was steaming and gurgling. My mother stood over it, watching to make sure it didn't boil over, holding her soup spoon at her side like a soldier holding her sword.

"Nikki's coming over, so we're gonna have to set a place for three," I said as I opened the fridge to grab a soda.

"Ah! Galileo, don't sneak up on me like that," my mother yelled, whipping around with her spoon in the air.

"Sorry, did you hear what I said about Nikki?"

"Oh, yes, we should be good. I made plenty of spaghetti."

With that, my mother went back to watching her cooking. While she finished up, I got to work getting out the plates, bowls, and silverware. At our house, we have a strange conglomeration of tableware. We have chopsticks, forks, spoons, knives, cheese knives, ice cream scoopers, nutcrackers, tuning forks, fondue forks, and skewers all in the same drawer. A typical family would keep their usual tableware in one drawer and everything else in another, right? Not our family. Mom insists that all of these objects are used for eating and should, therefore, be stored together. What's funny is watching her eat with a tuning

3

fork.

When I set the table, I make sure to grab what we need for whatever we're eating. If my Mom does it, there's no telling what she'll put on the table. You might end up with a punch bowl to eat your dinner out of with the fondue fork she brought you. That's why I like it better when I do it. A knock on the door alerted me of Nikki's arrival. Our doorbell doesn't work; we don't have enough visitors to warrant getting it fixed.

"I've got it," I said, leaving my mom to finish up the food.

Nikki is my best friend, but I have to say she's a total geek. She wears her curly hair up in two pigtails that look more like puff balls than anything, her two front teeth have a tiny gap between them, her bag is decorated in space memorabilia, and her clothes are always covered in alien propaganda. She's one of those who loves sci-fi movies and staying up late watching alien conspiracy videos. If I have to hear about the Roswell UFO one more time, I'll probably lose my mind.

"May I come in?" She asked, shuffling in place.

"If you aren't scared of getting probed," I teased.

Without a moment's hesitation, she stepped over the threshold of my house, taking off her shoes hurriedly. Nikki's Mom and dad own a company that does something with fuel, she explained it to me once, but I forgot. Her mom's the president and her dad's the CEO, so they're often out of town on business. It's not like they don't like her or anything, they just don't want their kids getting caught up in everything.

Nikki is the oldest of five, three boys and two girls, and they're all a different shade of dark. Nikki's the lightest, then her younger brother Dave, then John, then Sarah and Jamal are about the same. Her mother's pretty light and her dad's pretty dark, so some took after their mom and some their father. It

4

makes a lot of people question if they all have the same dad, but they do.

"I brought something sure to tell us if your mother is an alien," she whispered, checking to make sure my Mom was nowhere nearby.

"Oh god, what is it?"

Slowly, she pulled the device out from her bag, making sure to keep it hidden. It looked like a calculator and a GameBoy had a crack baby. There were all sorts of buttons and wires poking out in all directions. When she pushed the on button, the screen turned on, displaying nothing but white.

"What do you think?"

"I think you made someone on amazon very happy."

"Come on Galileo, this is the Invader Finder 2000, does that sound fake to you?"

"It sounds like your parents need to monitor your spending."

She didn't like that too much. As she glared at me, she pushed a button, and a tiny little blue dot appeared on the screen.

"This machine scans the area for aliens, if it senses one, the blue dot will turn red. It's supposed to do a bunch of other stuff, but I haven't figured it all out yet," she explained.

Of course she hadn't. More than likely it didn't have all the settings it claimed it did. She'd probably get home, push a button and it'd spit out the quadratic formula.

"Time for dinner," My Mom called.

"Let's take this baby for a test drive, shall we?" Nikki offered, proudly heading toward the kitchen.

Rolling my eyes, I followed behind her with my arms crossed. At least tonight I'm getting dinner and a show. The kitchen table was set with the large spaghetti pot in the center and the container of sauce sitting next to it. There was also a plate of buttered toast off to the side. My Mom noticed Nikki's little device immediately, but she didn't seem alarmed at all.

"Ooo, what's that?" She asked, taking her place at the table.

"It's a new game I bought," Nikki lied.

"That sounds fun."

There were no serving spoons or tongs for us to get our food with. Reaching into the pot, my mom grabbed a big handful of pasta and put it on her plate before dumping a load of sauce on top. Next to go for it was Nikki, after eating with us so many times, she was used to my mother's craziness. She kept the device hidden under the table in her lap, where she could check it occasionally during the meal.

Once everyone had gotten what they wanted, we started eating. While Nikki and I twirled our pasta into little bites around our fork, my mother grabbed at her pasta with her hands, shoving what she could into her mouth before slurping the rest up like slimy intestines. Her face was covered in red sauce after only a few bites, making her look like a cannibal.

"Thanks again for letting me join you, Ms. M."

"No problem Nikki. I don't mind at all. Speaking of, where'd your parents go this week?"

"France. There's supposed to be some big alternative fuel event going on," Nikki replied, glancing down.

"That sounds cool. Did they tell you what it was about?"

"The only thing I remember was that it had something to do with some old algae. I didn't really catch everything."

"Algae? That sounds so cool!" My Mom replied excitedly, placing her sauce-covered hands on the table.

"I guess."

Of course, the little light on Nikki's screen stayed blue no matter how close she got it to my mother. Occasionally it would beep, but that was about it, and it wasn't even loud enough to hear. It seemed she was getting desperate as she was trying to lean without looking suspicious.

"Say, Ms. M, wanna try my game out?" Nikki offered, holding out the little device.

My Mom tilted her head in curiosity, taking the device like it was a snake whose pattern she didn't recognize. I guess since it was coming from Nikki she trusted it. As soon as the little device passed from Nikki's hands, the dot turned bright red, then the entire screen turned to static before fading to all black.

"Oh no, I broke it!" My mother panicked.

"Don't worry about it, I'm sure I can get it working again," Nikki reassured her, trying to hide the triumphant grin on her face.

Groan, now I'm going to have to listen to her talk about how it's "proven" now. Rolling my eyes, I went back to eating my noodles. Sadly, Nikki proved my suspicions right, as soon as dinner ended, while my mother started cleaning up, she dragged me back to the living room with an insane look in her eyes. Once she made sure my mother hadn't followed, she pulled me down to sit next to her on the couch.

"Did you see that? Proof! Hard evidence. I can't wait until my fans hear about this."

Now when she says fans, she's referring to the 200 people that follow her blog on Tumblr, although I'm pretty sure at least a fourth of them are porn bots. She's continuously posting crazy stuff about Aliens on there, and she even has a whole segment dedicated to my Mom, but I refuse to read it. I'm scared to see what kind of crazy stuff she's done that I don't know about.

"Yeah, right. You saw how that thing was glitching out, it probably just short-circuited, and that's why the dot changed color," I explained.

"Come on, Stargazer, how come it only did that when I handed it to her? It didn't do that all throughout dinner, so what was different?" Nikki questioned.

It's hard to argue with her when she gets like this. No matter what I say, she's going to turn it down because she's already convinced herself, so I might as well just not even try.

"I don't know. Maybe keeping it on so long made it overheat or something? It was just a coincidence, don't get too excited."

"Yeah, right. You just want to ruin this for me," She said, already typing up a blog post on her phone.

"Would either of you like a cold cream sandwich?" My Mom said, appearing out of nowhere with three ice cream sandwiches in hand.

"Sure thing Ms. M," Nikki laughed, taking the sandwich that was closest to her.

I took the one in the middle, leaving the last one for my Mom, who happily took it and sat down in the empty recliner next to the couch. The three of us tore the packaging off and dug into our sweet treats. Nikki and I took our bites slowly, trying not to hurt our teeth from the cold, but my Mom ate the whole thing in just a few huge bites. She visibly cringed, but still continued to take massive bite after massive bite.

"I'll see you tomorrow, Gali. Thanks for letting me come over, Ms. M!"

Once she finished her ice cream, Nikki stood up to leave; her typical dine and dash maneuver. She had to be back home by a particular time, or the nanny would yell at her.

"No problem, my dear, feel free to come again," My mother offered.

"See you at school, tinfoil head."

8

Turning around, Nikki gave me the "loser" hand gesture before running off, nearly tripping on the uneven step that leads up to our front door. I headed up to my room after she left. Without her, I didn't really have a reason to be out among the living, so I retreated into my sanctuary.

My room is the only place in the house where everything makes sense. Unlike the rest of the home, it looks like a sane human being resides within. The walls are covered in posters of my favorite shows and bands, my desk is neat and organized with my laptop in the middle, my clothes are put up, and my bed has matching pillows and bedding. It's not a huge room, but there's plenty of space for me to be me.

The bed creaked loudly when I flopped onto it. I pulled my phone out, plugged my headphones in, and turned on some of my favorite music. Personally, I prefer Techno, but I'm not opposed to a good rap song every once in a while, it all depends on what kind of mood I'm in, and right now I'm in a techno mood.

As my ears were filled with fun technological sounds, I stared up at the ceiling, thinking about Nikki's stupid device. Not gonna lie, it was odd that it messed up right when my Mom touched it, but that doesn't really mean anything. That was a piece of junk anyway. My Mom may be weird, but that doesn't make her an alien.

2

Chapter 2

I knew Nikki wasn't going to let that stupid button thing go. She had the most annoying grin on her face when I saw her at school first thing in the morning. I had hoped to avoid her until her excitement fizzled out, but she caught me at lunch.

"Guess what Starboy, our little experiment last night earned me 5 more followers. My post got 30 notes, a new record for me, so suck it."

"Just because it's popular doesn't make it factual," I countered.

"I figured you'd say something like that, so let me point out, one of those notes came from the official blog for the hit tv show 'Invaders In My Backyard,' and they said I should send them a statement," She declared proudly, her hands on her hips.

"Did they also ask for your credit card number?"

"No, you moron, they have a tv show, they don't need money."

She obviously didn't get my joke. Pulling out her phone, she tried to show me, but I couldn't follow anyway, there were so many words sprinkled throughout that only conspiracy theorists know. As soon as I saw the word "Illuminati," I had to look away. Nikki's my best friend, but there's only so much tinfoil hat-edness I can handle in one day.

"I looked it up, and my Invader Finder has so many more functions for me to try. There's one function where it will emit a low-frequency noise that only aliens can hear. The sound drives them nuts, so if one is nearby, they'll reveal themselves when they cover their ears!"

"So it's a dog whistle," I interrupted.

"Dog whistles are high-frequency, dumb ass."

"Hey, I'm not a dog expert, just like how you aren't an expert on alien biology."

She was too absorbed in her phone to hear me, rolling my eyes, I went back to my lunch. I still had a whole chicken sandwich to eat, I wasn't about to let her conspiracies get in the way of that. School lunch may not be that great, but it's food, and I'm hungry. Nikki never eats lunch at school. She says the government saves the more unsavory ingredients to feed to the students since it's cheaper than using the nicer ones. This sandwich may be made out of chicken ears and toenails, but I'm too hungry to care, use enough ketchup, and anything's edible.

One thing that I don't understand is that she refuses to eat the school food, which is definitely made by human lunch ladies, but she trusts anything my mom makes, and she thinks she's an alien. She's always talking about Aliens implanting probes in our food to take us over from the inside, how is my mom any different? Maybe she's scared of insulting her. I mean, if aliens do end up coming and mom really is an alien, she'll be Nikki's one-way ticket to unlocking the secrets she speculates about online. As if that would ever happen.

The sound of the bell had us all getting up and heading to class like the trained sheep we are. You see, Nikki and I make great friends because the two of us like to rebel. She loves to rebel against what's normal, while I rebel against authority. Every now and then, our arguments cross, and we make an excellent team, but usually, it's just the two of us ranting to each other.

I had my favorite class; politics, right after lunch, a real disservice if you ask me. With my stomach full, I always ended up getting really sleepy, which made it hard to pay attention, but I want to so badly.

I guess you can say that in Politics I'm the snarky teacher's pet. I sit at the front, take detailed notes, and raise my hand to answer every question; right if I may add. Nikki's the same way, but in astronomy, so we help each other study. We swap notes after school and take them home to study. Sometimes she'll come over to my house, and we'll have a cram sesh in my living room. We would have it at her place, but her siblings would never leave us alone long enough to get anything done.

The politics teacher here at Bridgewood High is a short man named Mr. Leery. He's got a messy looking brown comb-over, small round-rimmed glasses, a beer belly that sways back and forth when he walks, and a mean disposition towards any student that doesn't do well in his class, which is pretty much everyone. In his mind, if a student fails his course, it's not because he did a lousy job teaching, but instead they did a horrible job receiving. He's a jerk, but I love the challenge. Seeing his frustration as I ace each quiz he makes no matter how difficult he makes them makes it all worth it.

"Good afternoon Galileo," He sneers at me as I take my place. "Same to you, Leery."

He hates when I call him by just his last name. The best part is, he can report me to the principle as many times he wants, but calling a teacher by their name is not against any rules.

The class starts the same every day, with a ridiculously hard warm-up that he found on the internet and edited to make even harder. The goal isn't for you to get it right, it's for you to get it wrong so he can condescendingly explain it to the entirety of the class, but I always ruin that for him. As the other kids start to panic and grab the nearest textbook, I calmly read the question and write down the answer.

"Remember, students, we talked about this last week."

We really didn't, we talked about Political Alignments last week, but this question is about Voting. The two are related, but certainly not in a way that would make sense to your average student. Lucky for me, I'm not your average student.

"Times up, does anyone have the answer?"

The usual silence filled the class as everyone waited, hoping someone else would have the answer so he wouldn't start calling on people. It's a dangerous game they play, but that's why there are people like me, to bail them out. Proudly I raised my hand, a defiant look on my face.

"Galileo," Mr. Leery said with a sigh.

"The answer is Gerrymandering. The method used to unfairly draw voting districts is called Gerrymandering."

"Correct," Mr. Leery groaned.

A collective sigh of relief spread through the class as the other students realized they were safe from being called on. It was clear on Mr. Leery's face that he was disappointed that he didn't get a chance to embarrass anyone. With that, he pulled up today's lesson and started teaching. Near about the middle of class, my phone buzzed with a text from Nikki.

"Reconnaissance, tonight, 17:00. Bring accouterments." Translation, "Need a brainstorming sesh tonight. I'll be there at five. Bring Snacks, ".

13

Mom was supposed to be working the night shift tonight, so I can go there for the snacks.

"Sounds good. Any special requests?" I texted back.

"Excuse me, Galileo! You may not need to pay attention, but I would appreciate it if you wouldn't text while I'm talking."

Crap, I was caught.

"Sorry. I was texting my mom."

"It can wait until school ends, can't it?"

"Yes, sir."

I put away my phone to satisfy Mr. Leery. He'd probably give me detention if I didn't, then I wouldn't be able to be home by five if I stopped for snacks. After giving me a healthy stink eye, he turned around to continue his lesson.

The bell had hardly finished ringing before I took off towards the convenience store. I was ready to go twenty minutes before that, but they took a while to ring the bell, something about the buses not being there yet or whatever.

It was only a ten-minute walk from Bridgewood to the store, five if you run. The stroll took you right through the busiest parts of town, which still weren't that busy. One of the downsides of living in a small town; it's super bland. Yes, I can get anywhere in a matter of minutes, yes, the traffic is never a problem, but at the same time, there's nothing exciting going on. On the weekends, the coolest thing you can do is maybe go to the movies, and even then, the theater in town is only ever showing three films at a time since it's so small.

On the way, I passed the barber's shop, the only diner in town, the grocery store, and the tailor before I reached my destination, MeMe's Pitstop, one of the oldest buildings in town. The gas station out front is 10 years newer than the actual convenience store. Before that, MeMe's was a little shop that sold everything you could possibly need. A little while after the new owner took over, he added a fuel station out front in the hopes of boosting business.

The little bell on top of the door jingled as I pushed it open. I come in here so often, you'd think I'd hear that bell in my sleep.

"Welcome to MeMe's," My mom called from her spot at the register.

She was busy ringing someone up, so she didn't notice it was me.

"Hey, mah!" I called, grabbing the first bag of tasty looking chips that I saw.

"Hey baby, what are you here for today?" She replied, finishing up.

"Some snacks. Nikki's coming over to study."

"Don't stay up too late. I'll be home around ten."

Mom was talking to me, but I wasn't really listening. I was too busy thinking about the best snacks to get to both limit costs and get all we wanted. Nikki likes Barbeque chips, so I grabbed a bag of off-brand. We both like Oreos, so I got a thing of those. I got a big bag of caramel popcorn for me since I'll probably eat the whole thing myself. With snacks covered, I moved over to the drinks section. Nikki likes Coke, and I like Dr. Pepper, so I got two bottles of each.

"There's leftover spaghetti in the fridge if you get hungry," Mom said as she rang me up.

"Sounds good to me. I'll save you some."

"Don't worry about me, I can make a sandwich if I need to."

Mom shares her employee discount with me, so all the stuff I got only cost me a little over ten bucks. One of my mom's coworkers came walking up after I handed her the cash.

"Hey, Matilda. Can you help me? I can't get the hot dog

machine to come back on."

"Sure. Bye, baby, see you when I get home," My mom said, running off to fix the machine.

Nikki beat me to the house, but I think she got there early on purpose. She was already "scanning" my place with her little device when I walked up.

"Found anything?" I asked, startling her.

"Not yet, but I didn't really expect to. An alien would keep their things hidden inside."

"Then why were you scanning?"

"Because, you never know what she might have slipped up on," Nikki replied matter of factly, putting up her weird gadget.

Her bag bounced as she straightened up, nearly falling off her shoulder. She let it hang loosely on her body, getting in her way as she looked down at her phone.

"You going to unlock the door or not?"

"Relax."

The keys on my keychain were color-coded, but they didn't really need to be, I only had three. One for my house, one for my lockbox, and one for the shed in the garden. My house key is green, like cartoon aliens. Nikki quickly went and jumped on my couch once I got the door open. She plopped her feet on one end, setting her bag on the ground next to her. Giving a grand sigh, she stretched her arms. The two of us pulled out the books for our respective classes, laying them out in front of the other. We have a unique method of studying. We read each other's notes and ask questions if we need to, but we don't follow along with each other. It's not precisely studying "together," but more like studying in the vicinity of the other.

We are masters at decoding each other's handwriting. Five years of reading each other's notes will do that to you. My notes are excellent and organized, making it easy for me to follow, while Nikki's are all over the place, scattered between doodles and plans, but I've learned how to pick out the essential bits. I was having a hard time understanding the whole concept of how light waves curve as they travel certain distances, but the way Nikki put it made it much easier to understand. She related it to how light bends in a pool or when it creates a rainbow. Now that I knew that, the math made a lot more sense.

"Hey Gali, I've got a new experiment planned. Want to join?" Nikki asked, not looking up.

"Depends, what is it?"

"Well, I've been reading about radio waves and how they travel through space. I bought a really powerful radio online, which should be arriving soon. I think I'm going to point it towards space to see if I hear anything," She explained while rewriting my notes.

"That sounds ridiculous. What do you think you're going to hear besides space noise?"

"If an intelligent life form is passing by looking for other intelligent life forms through radio, I'll be able to hear them and invite them to Earth. I could make the first contact for humanity."

My notes were now lying abandoned, she was too busy talking about her plans with a wicked look in her eyes.

"How long are you going to do it for? It's not every day that an intelligent life form passes by," I rebuked.

"I'll do it every night, after school. I can record it and post it on my blog. Maybe my fans will hear something that I don't."

"Yeah, right. All you'll hear is space noise and maybe a passing satellite," I teased, taking a sip of my soda.

"Whatever, when I'm on the news, you'll be sorry."

She says stuff like that a lot. She's obsessed with the idea that one day she'll prove aliens are real and get famous. Honestly, I think if she ends up on the news, it'll be for breaking into area 51. There were no snacks left when we finished our cramming session. I was almost done with my second soda when Nikki shut her books and stood up.

"Good work, Stargazer. I'll see you tomorrow."

"Same to you tinfoil head," I called as she walked out the door with her things in tow.

She left me to clean everything up, revenge for making fun of her. Despite them being off-brand, she had happily gobbled down the barbeque chips. There was only one Oreo left, which I ate before tossing the container away. My papers were spread all over the place, so I had to put everything back together before cramming it all in my bag.

I wasn't that hungry, but I still heated up a bowl of spaghetti for myself, tucking into it as I watched cartoons on the couch. Mom wasn't home yet when I went to bed, but it was close to when she said she'd be back. I made sure the door was locked before tucking myself into bed. Nikki had texted me to let me know she was home, so I sent back a quick "k."

3

Chapter 3

It was a good thing we had that study session last night. I got a flat 80 on the astronomy test, and I'm pretty sure the teacher was being generous. I'm betting that, if I hadn't studied, I would have gotten a 65. Of course, Nikki got a 98.

"Seasons do last 21 years on Uranus! I've got to talk to her about that," She complained to me at lunch.

A 98 isn't good enough for her, not in her favorite class. In any other category, she would have been ok with a 98, but because it was astronomy, she refused to settle for anything less than perfection.

"By the way, watch out for Leery, I got an 85 on that test," She said, fiddling around with her phone.

"Did you forget who you're talking to? I'm Gali freaking leo, Politics can suck my dick," I replied jokingly.

"If it could find it."

I gave her a friendly punch on the shoulder, my only rebuttal. She punched me back, laughing and leaning over.

"By the way, I'll be at your place tonight at 5:30. I figured out how to make my Invader Finder make that special noise I was telling you about, and I'm ready to test it out."

"Have you ever been to my house for something other than an experiment or a study session?" I teased.

"Don't forget the food. I come over for food a lot."

"Right. You only come to my house when you want something," I corrected.

"Ding ding ding, give the man a prize. Why else would I come over Space Cadet?"

"To hang out, like normal kids."

"But we aren't normal kids. Why would we try to pretend?" She asked, looking up at me with one eyebrow raised, finally ignoring her phone.

"Hey, fake it till you make it," I replied, hoping to lighten the mood. It seemed to work, since she giggled and looked back down at her phone.

The bell rang not long after, sending us all to our next class.

Every desk in Leery's room was covered in notes and textbooks, as frantic students tried to cram as much studying in as they could before Leery finally made them put their things away. In a total power move, I walked in and sat down, not pulling out my notes or anything. Confidently, I sat at my desk with my hands folded, waiting for the test to be passed out.

The test was several pages stapled together, the usual for politics. We had a bubble sheet to fill in our answers, and that was it. Leery prefers the bubble sheets, it makes it easier for him to grade, and besides, he doesn't give us free-response questions on the tests.

All the tests in his class are harder than warm-ups and the stuff we had learned that unit. I guess he thinks that since we have the basics, we'll be able to apply it to bigger and better things, but that's not always true. If it weren't for my skill in politics, I'm pretty sure I'd have a C in here.

As usual, I'm the first one done. In other classes, I'll wait until someone else turns their test in to turn in mine, but not in Politics. The look on Mr. Leery's face as I turn in my test before anyone else, finished in a matter of minutes, gives me such satisfaction. It almost makes the class worth it. Since I'd finished my test, I pulled my phone out to let my mom know Nikki was coming.

"Hey Mom, Nikki's coming over tonight. Cool?" I typed.

"Sure, Bby. Your Friends' r always whalecome." She replied.

My poor mother, she can speak easily, but her spelling is a bit rough. She spells it like she hears it, and that's part of the problem. I've thought about buying her some books on English, but I never get around to doing it. I mean, she doesn't type a lot at work, and she can read, so she's functional, she just messes up when she's writing or typing.

"Thanks, mom!"

":3 <3."

She can use symbols pretty well, so I often get cutesy little messages made up of them. I've tried to show her emojis, but she likes to make her own. There was still a good thirty minutes left, so I pulled up one of the games on my phone and started to fiddle around. I play a lot of resource farming and fighting games, it's fun to watch your resources grow depending on how you allocate them. Nikki likes to play mindless games with no goal to pass the time. I can see why she likes them, but they just aren't my style. About 15 minutes until class was over, my phone beeped with a text.

"Mission control to space cadet. What's the 411?" It was from Nikki, of course, the only person besides my mom that texts me regularly.

"Already finished. Just waiting for Leery to admit defeat and hand me my 100."

"Please limit the smugness space cadet."

"You're just jealous. Here he comes ;>."

With an annoyed look on his face, Mr. Leery planted my test face down roughly on my desk. As he left to hand the next student theirs, I flipped mine over, revealing the lovely red 100 at the top of the page.

"See?" I sent her, accompanied by a photo of my test.

The little cloud of her typing popped up for a second then disappeared as she likely put her phone away in frustration. She may have me beat in astronomy, but I crush her when it comes to Politics. I was already ready to leave when the bell rang. I had my bag around my shoulder, and all I had to do was stuff my phone in my pocket for the long trek.

My usual path takes me through the center of town, taking about 15 minutes for me to get home. I don't pass the convenience store when I go this way, though, which is only a problem when I want to get snacks. There was a slight breeze, cutting through the heat and cooling me off, making the walk sufferable.

In the summer, I have a hard time walking home. Sometimes I'll take the bus; otherwise, I'll stroll around and stop somewhere for a drink to keep myself from dropping from a heat stroke. It'd be nice if mom could get a car. Then she could come pick me up, or I could get my license and drive myself. The only problem is, mom is terrified of vehicles that run on fossil fuel. She's ok with solar-powered cars, but not ones that run on gasoline. I think wherever she came from had more primitive forms of transport that relied on something other than fossil fuel, and that's why she's so scared. That's probably why she's so interested in what Nikki's parents do.

Nikki is convinced that the reason she's scared of fossil fuels is that the planet she's from relied on some super-advanced form of fuel and sees things like gasoline as barbaric and dangerous. I don't buy it. Maybe over the summer I'll get a job and save up for a down payment on a car. Then my mom could pay the monthly fee with her paycheck, and we could share it. She wouldn't have to ride her bike everywhere, and I wouldn't have to always walk. I'll have to tell her about my idea later tonight.

Tonight for dinner, my mother had decided on chicken and french fries that she bought from the store. I could smell it cooking when I opened the door.

"I'm home!" I called, tossing my bag to the ground.

"Welcome back," My mom replied from the kitchen.

When I walked in, she was sitting right in front of the oven, watching intently with her legs crossed. The oven has a timer on it, but she doesn't trust it. Even though the side of the bag clearly tells you how long to cook everything for, she doesn't believe it and insists on watching the food cook. I told her that a group of food scientists or whatever got together and determined the best time to cook the food for based on experimentation, but that means nothing to her apparently.

"How's dinner going?" I asked, going to get the dinnerware.

"Good, I think it's getting close to being done. Could you get out the ketchup?" She replied.

"Sure. Anything else?" "Mayo, if you want it."

Personally, I don't like mayo. On sandwiches, it's not bad, but that's about the extent of that. I'll eat it on a burger, depending on the burger, but Nikki loves the stuff. She likes to mix ketchup and mayo and dip her fries in it. She'll put it on sandwiches, burgers, hot dogs, just about anything. Mom will occasionally dip her fries in the ketchup mayo mix to see what all the hype is about, but she usually, like me, prefers just plain ketchup.

As I set up three place settings, I noticed mom opening the oven. Using a spatula, she pushed the chicken and fries around to inspect them. Seemingly satisfied, she set down the spatula and reached inside. She grabs the pan with her bare hands, pulling it out and closing the door behind her with her leg. It wasn't until I was about 13 that I learned you're not supposed to just grab the pan. I had always seen mom do it, so I figured that was how everyone did. It wasn't until Nikki came over and screamed when she saw it that I learned it wasn't normal. When I asked her about it, she said she has powerful hands from years of hard labor, and that's why she doesn't feel it. It makes sense to me.

The doorbell rang not long after mom had finished seasoning the fries.

"I've got it," I called, jogging toward the front door.

Standing in the doorway, looking exactly like she did at school, backpack and all, was none other than Nikki. I had expected her to run home and drop off her bag, but I guess she didn't.

"I didn't get a chance to change, I was busy chasing a squirrel that I suspect was secretly an alien in disguise," She said, kicking off her shoes.

"What gave you that impression?"

"It kept making noises at me, likely asking me to take it to our leader."

"It probably just wanted a peanut."

Nikki waved me off, looking down at her weird Invader Finder thing.

"Quiet Starboy. Tonight is a night of discovery. If this works,

24

we will know for certain if your mother is an alien or not!" She declared, hitting a button on the side of the device.

The screen changed to show a little logo of sound waves coming out of the speaker, letting the user know that it was emitting the frequency. I didn't hear anything, and neither did Nikki, so we just had to trust that it was working.

"Alright, let's go."

Mom was setting down a spatula to pick up the food with when we walked in. Her head came up, looking around for something.

"Do you two hear that?" She asked, raising an eyebrow.

Nikki's face lit up. She looked over at me with a huge shit-eating grin. I rolled my eyes, a bit surprised, but still not fully believing.

"No, what does it sound like Ms. M?"

"It sounds like, it sounds like…" My mom muttered, turning toward the window in front of the sink.

Leaning over, she opened it, revealing a baby blue jay sitting in a nest on the windowsill. Although its eyes were closed, it turned toward the noise and opened its mouth, chirping for food.

"It's about time you hatched. I was beginning to wonder if the frost had gotten to you," My mom cooed, closing the window back.

Nikki's grin disappeared, while one found its way to my face. She had so much faith in that little box of hers, it's funny watching it all go up in flames.

"Let's eat, you two," My mom chirped.

We all scooped up a bunch of chicken and fries, placing them on our plates before reaching for the condiments. Like I suspected, Nikki took the mayo and ketchup to mix the two together, making a peachy colored sauce that she happily dipped her chicken and fries in. Mom was the last to get some ketchup, she poured way too much onto her plate and started scooping it up with fries like salsa. She did the same with the chicken, covering her face in the sauce.

"How was school today, you guys?" Mom asked, breaking the silence.

"It was good. We had a test in astronomy and another in politics," Nikki answered.

"Ooo, tell me about it!" Mom yelled, excitedly leaning forward.

The two of them leaned aside to talk about astronomy, leaving their food unattended. This arrangement works great, Nikki likes to talk about astronomy, and mom likes to learn about it, it's perfect. While they spoke, I swiped a tender off Nikki's plate.

Nikki stayed long enough to help us clean up before heading toward the door. She told my mom goodbye then gestured for me to follow. As she put on her shoes, she looked me in the eye, leaning against the wall.

"I started the radio experiment last night," She began.

"And?""I didn't get anything, but I'm hopeful. If I wait long enough, I'll get something, even if it's just a passing comet."

"What makes you think you could hear a comet on a radio?"

"I'd be able to hear the interference, stop asking questions. If I hear anything, I'm going to ask your mother to translate."

She had her shoes on at this point and was standing with her hands on her book bag straps.

"What makes you think she will just so happen to speak the language that the aliens that you hear are speaking?"

"Alien society is probably light years ahead of us, so they

26

probably grow up learning several languages, or maybe she had access to an alien database that has all sorts of languages cataloged. I don't know."

"Well then, don't bank on it," I teased, leaning against the door frame.

"Whatever, see you, Starchild."

That's a new one.

"See you, tin foil head."

I'm going to have to think of some new ones. She's got so many for me, I need to get on the ball with that one. Drinker of the Kool-aid is a bit much, plus it's not very clear. I'll have to get more creative.

4

Chapter 4

Weekends are my favorite time of the week. In fact, I know very few people who dislike weekends. The ones who do probably have to work on them or something. Typically, on any given Saturday, you'll find me sitting in my bed playing on my phone with the fan turned up high. For hours I'll watch youtube videos, stream movies, or listen to music while staring straight up with my arms spread out like Jesus.

Sometimes Mom has to work on Saturdays. Those days I'll migrate from my cave to the living room couch and watch tv or eat three bowls of cereal with my shirt off. Today was not one of those days. She was sitting in the living room downstairs doing whatever it is that she does. We spend time together sometimes, but not all the time, that would just be weird. I like movie nights the best. We make popcorn, pile on the couch, and watch a movie we either rented online or from Redbox. By the end, there'll be popcorn everywhere, the two of us having tossed it for one reason or another. Movie nights are scheduled for the third Saturday of every month, but we do spontaneous ones sometimes. There's no rule against more than one movie night a month, there just has to be at least one.

"Galileo!" My mom called from downstairs.

It wasn't the third Saturday, so it may or may not be about a movie night. Only one way to be sure.

"Yes?" I called back.

"Come here."

"Yes, Ma'am."

I got up and headed downstairs, putting my phone away. More than likely, she had found a movie that she wanted to watch with me, inspiring an impromptu movie night. She probably needed my help making popcorn and grabbing a soda. When I made it downstairs, though, she was sitting on the couch with her phone in her hand, a big smile on her face.

"Galileo, I've good news!" She cheered.

"What is it?"

"My boss just emailed me, he's giving me a raise! Let's go out to celebrate."

Mom hasn't gotten a raise in a long time. This is awesome! Maybe now, with the extra money, I can convince her to get a car. I'll wait to bring that up, though, until she receives a paycheck or two. That way, I'll have a little something to back me up.

"Awesome! Where do you want to go?"

"What about Hanabi?" She suggested.

"Sounds good to me. I'll go get ready."

Knowing we'd be walking, I put on some comfy shoes and some loose clothes. Mom was already waiting by the door once I'd finished. She had on her trademark baggy clothes and tennis shoes. When she doesn't have to work, she dresses very comfortably in things like sweatpants and t-shirts. She dresses

29

more like a broke college student than someone's mom, but it is what it is. It's a long walk to the Hibachi place. It's on the outskirts of town, closer to where most people live.

A lot of people were shocked when they started to build the place. It's so rare for a new building to be built around here, so the whole town was interested. People would come and stand on the sidewalk just watching them build. Of course, everyone started to try and guess what they were making. The most popular guesses were bank or jailhouse, but that changed as the building began to come together. Everyone figured out it was going to be a restaurant, but they weren't sure what kind. When the builders started to work on the koi pond outside, we all knew what it was.

Hanabi is one of the most delightful restaurants around. The outside is heavily influenced by Japanese architecture, and it has a cute firework theme. Bright lights on the side of the building reflect off the water, giving the place a beautiful shimmering effect. There's a covered part outside right next to the koi pond where you can sit and eat. If there's any space open, mom insists on sitting there. She likes to sit and try to talk to the fish, and today is no different.

"You've gotten bigger!" She said as a bright yellow koi swam by.

"How do you know it's the same one?" I ask, taking a sip from my drink.

"Because he's the only one with pure yellow scales. The other yellow one has that pretty black pattern overlaid," she replied matter of factly.

A small white and orange one came swimming by us, prompting mom to sit up and lean over the edge.

"A baby! That's a new one," she yelled excitedly.

30

All around us, people turned to look at the crazy lady yelling about a fish. I covered my face in embarrassment, silently praying that none of the people here knew who I was.

"You're going to be so pretty when you grow up," mom said, waving goodbye to the tiny thing as it swam around the corner.

"Have you two decided what you want?" The waitress asked, startling the both of us.

"Oh! Yes, ma'am, we have."

"Alright, what would you two like?"

"Hibachi steak, clear soup, and ranch dressing on the salad," my mom relayed.

We get the same thing every time we come here. If you sit outside, they don't cook it in front of you, so it's a little cheaper, plus the fire stresses mom out. All my friends tell me how cool it is, maybe one day I'll go with them and get to watch it.

I told the waitress my order then went back to playing on my phone. She smiled and said she'd be back with our soup in a moment. The soup here may not look that exciting, but it's so good. Our waitress comes back and sets down two little bowls full of liquid right in front of us, the salads coming right after. There are small bits of green onion and mushroom floating in the light yellow liquid, the steam from it hitting my nose, bringing the light, salty scent right to me.

As I pick up the flat bottomed spoon, mom looks at me, confused.

"I've forgotten, is it noodles or soup that you're supposed to slurp?" She asked.

"Depends on the culture. Here you're supposed to slurp the soup, it helps cool it down. You can slurp the noodles, but it makes it kind of messy," I replied, slurping down a spoonful.

"You're so smart, Galileo! Must be that schooling. Isn't it

31

wonderful? I wish I could have gone to school when I was younger," She praised before picking up her bowl and slurping away.

"I learned that bit online," I corrected.

"Online? The internet certainly is wonderful, isn't it?"

I was fortunate with mom. Unlike other moms who try to limit the time their children spend online, she encourages me to spend as much time as I want on it. She is amazed by the idea of a free database full of information that anyone can access, so she insists I take full advantage. Our salads didn't last long once the soup ran out. They're pretty small, not meant to fill you up before your dinner, but man, they do hit the spot. It's a sweet little refreshing snack before the big meal.

We were taking the last bite of our salad when the food came. The waitress set down two big identical plates full of food. Here you get fried rice and veggies with your meat on top of the soup and salad. They also have sushi, but mom doesn't trust raw fish. The waitresses always bring you a pair of chopsticks with your food. I guess it's so nobody gets offended, thinking they assumed that you couldn't use them. You also get a fork, spoon, and knife, so you're fine if you haven't mastered it, just yet, or if you're pretty good but hate trying to eat rice with them. I've been practicing lately.

They make a beautiful wooden snap sound as I break them apart. I poise one between my thumb and the side of my hand and hold the other with my forefinger and thumb. I give that one an experimental lift up and down before going after a tasty looking veggie and piece of meat. Luckily, I didn't drop it, popping it proudly into my mouth. Mom tried to mimic what I was doing, but she never can hold them steady. Usually, she'll drop one, or they'll be crooked as she tries to grab something.

With a bit more practice, I bet she could do it.

"I can't get it, Galileo. Could you show me again?"

"Of course, mom," I reply, reaching out to help her.

She almost had it, but her chopstick wasn't quite firmly held by her thumb. I shifted it down and readjusted the one in her fingers. It looked like she had it, so I backed up and allowed her to try it out. Rather than going for a smaller piece that would have required more skill, I pointed to a bigger portion of meat for her to go for. She was a bit wobbly, but she managed to get it into her mouth.

"You're so talented, Gali. Thank you so much."

"Don't worry about Ma. Thanks for taking me out to eat."

She went back to using her fork incorrectly, but at least she had managed to use the chopsticks once. Maybe that'll be one utensil that she'll use adequately.

Dinner was delicious, as usual. The sun finally set as we were eating, making the bright lights look even more brilliant. Now the lights dancing on the walls looked even more defined. The brighter ones managed to penetrate the water, splashing color on all the koi, making them look like rainbow fish. While mom paid, I watched the fish swim around, trying to follow them on their journey.

One of the benefits of living in a small town is there isn't a lot of light pollution so at night we can see tons of stars in the sky. Mom used to love taking me stargazing in the park. We'd lay there and point at the constellations, making up names and stories for them all. In astronomy, I have a hard time referring to them as their actual names since I've always known them by the ones we made up.

"Hey mom, do you remember the wayward traveler?" I asked, looking up at one constellation in particular.

"Of course, with his traveling belt," she replied, looking at the same stars.

"I found out in school that he's actually called Orion, a hunter."

"Really? So rather than idealizing the pursuit of knowledge, we've chosen to immortalize a violent and outdated tradition?" My mom asked, perplexed.

"Well, back when astronomers first started naming the constellations, being a hunter was a more popular occupation. It was more lucrative and sustainable than it is now," I replied.

"Hmm, interesting. Funny how things have changed since then. Maybe they should rename all the constellations, give them more modern titles. Ones that reflect society's current values."

"Maybe. Hey, we should write down our names and send them to NASA, they might like them enough to adopt them," I joked.

"I'd rather they stay between us. Something special between mother and son so that every time you look up at the night sky, you remember the stories we made up together all those years ago."

"Yeah, that would kind of spoil it. Do you remember the story of the wounded soldier?"

"How could I forget? The soldier, wounded from his battle, grabbed a comet and soared toward Earth. He was so close, but the comet told him it didn't want it's journey to end, so all it could do was leave him up in the sky. When the soldier let go, the comet continued soaring on, leaving him trapped alone out in space. However, he still points toward his home, hoping someone on Earth will take him home one day," mom repeated for the hundredth time probably.

"That one's my favorite. Hey, do you ever want to go back

home? Maybe one day you could take me there," I offered.

Mom turned to look at me with a stern look on her face. Her eyes looked glossy, but that might have just been the lighting.

"Baby, I was running from something bigger than you could imagine. Unless things get better, I don't want you anywhere near my home, okay?"

"Okay, but it's a shame. I'd love to learn more about where I come from."

"That's not important. What matters is where you are now," she replied, all philosophical like.

Damn, I was trying to probe her, but it seems she didn't take the bait. She's always so touchy when I talk about where she immigrated from, she won't even tell me. Still, once I saw her write "Malaysia" on a document. I don't know if that's exactly where she's from, but it's something. We went straight to bed when we got home, completely full and tired from our walk. It was a nice change of pace.

5

Chapter 5

Booting up the cheap camera I had attached to my laptop, I did a last-minute check of my radio system. All of the lights seemed to be on, and I could hear a slight humming sound.

When the recording program I use booted up, I took a moment to make sure I looked alright. My hair was in its usual dual puffs, and I had on my favorite leather jacket covered in alien patches. It's not necessarily professional, but it totally goes well with what I'm doing. Taking a deep breath, I hit record.

"Hey there, my fellow believers! It's ya girl, Nikki, back with day 17 of our little radio experiment. So far, we've managed to capture 8 satellites, 32 meteors, and one potential comet although we're not sure. You can listen to those on my page under the Space Audio post. Now, are you all ready to listen?"

These streams would be super boring if all I did was sit here with the radio playing nonsense, so to keep things interesting, I tell stories about Galileo's mom, but I always make sure not to give away any identifying details. Those are the most popular thing on my page. People love following my adventures as I try to uncover the truth. Some of my bigger fans even help me come up with new ways to experiment.

"Tonight's topic is one that I find incredibly intriguing. Are aliens allergic to bees? You may be wondering where I came up with this idea, but I promise it is not baseless. Yesterday, my class went on a field trip to a farm to learn about farming and stuff like that. You all remember my friend's mom, the suspected alien, anyway, she was chaperoning this particular trip. While we were walking outside, past a bunch of goats, a few bees started flying around us. My friend's mom freaked, running around and screaming at the top of her lungs. This might have just been a simple case of bee phobia, but I think-"

I was in the middle of my story, when I heard the slightest noise coming from the radio. It was incredibly faint, but it was there, and it wasn't just a regular interference.

"Hold on guys, do you hear that?" I asked the camera, leaning towards the radio.

It came again, just the tiniest bit louder. I wasn't sure, but it sounded like a woman's voice calling for someone. No matter how long I waited, the voice didn't get any louder. In the stream chat, a few people were arguing about what they were hearing. A few were convinced that they heard someone saying "help," but others said they heard "come in." They were both totally different phrases, though, so I had no idea. Those who weren't debating were just calling it fake, saying they didn't even hear anything, the usual disbeliever crap.

"I don't know what to say, guys. That's definitely not a meteor. It's too articulate just to be any old interference, and it's not clear enough to be coming from Earth."

I fiddled with the knobs, causing the radio to jump from station to station, each one loud and crisp, but when I switched

37

back to space, that tiny little noise was still there.

"It's been going on for too long. If it were just an oddly sounding interference, it should have stopped by now. Any object would have burned up in the atmosphere. This is weird, guys."

My heart was racing, my palms growing sweaty as thoughts ran through my head at a million miles an hour. Is this the first contact? Have I really managed to pick up an alien craft trying to make contact with Earth?

"It's not getting louder, maybe they're too far away? I'll check in again tomorrow. Sorry for cutting this episode short, guys, but I really don't know where to go from here. I'll get back to you guys soon. Keep your eyes on the stars!" I signed off.

I turned off the stream before downloading the video. I always upload them to youtube so anyone who couldn't watch it live can still watch it. Tomorrow night I'll isolate the sound I was hearing, amplify it, and upload it to my space noise post. This one is bigger than I ever could have imagined, I have to tell Galileo. Before I went to bed, I shut down the radio, the noise still playing out of its speakers.

The next day, I had a hard time hiding my excitement. I wanted to scream to the world what I'd found, but I kept quiet. If it gets out that I made first contact, I could end up in some pretty hot water. The only person I trusted not to rat me out was Galileo. He risked exposing his mom as an alien so he'd keep my secret.

As soon as I got to lunch, I went looking for him. He had beat me there and was already eating the nasty school food. I ran over and slammed my hands down in front of him, shaking his tray.

"Someone's excited," Galileo commented, taking a sip of his

milk.

"Look, I'm onto something big. If I tell you, you can't tell a soul," I whispered, looking over my shoulders.

"I haven't reported you as a mental case yet, I think you can trust me," He joked.

"This isn't the time to be making jokes. Our lives could be on the line."

Galileo clearly was not taking this seriously at all. He looked at me with a blank expression, like I'd just told him I was going to explain how rain works. For a moment, I doubted my decision to tell him, but if there's anyone I know who should know this, it's him.

"Last night, I heard something, no someone, trying to make contact," I whispered.

"What'd they say? For a great low rate, you can get online?"

"Haha, very funny. No, I couldn't tell what they were saying exactly, but I think it was important."

"Why would Aliens be broadcasting important information for anyone to intercept?"

"I don't mean war codes important, but maybe missing person important."

His expression wasn't quite as doubtful anymore, but he still looked at me like I was talking about rocks or something. Maybe I could win him over if I showed him a clip from last night's video.

"Here. Look at this."

I pulled my phone out, quickly pulling up my Tumblr and scrolling down to the post. I wasn't sure exactly when the noise started, I just blindly scrolled around until I got to the point where I was talking about it to the camera. After plugging my headphones in, I handed my phone to Galileo shoving a headphone in his ear, keeping the other for myself. You could just barely hear the noise over me talking, but it was clearly there. When I paused to listen in the video, you could hear it even better. Man, I'm glad I sprung for a better mic last month. With a big grin on my face, I looked at him excitedly, hoping to see him look back with an equally excited expression, but instead, he just raised his brow at me.

"What?"

"What?! What do you mean what? You hear it, right? Proof! Proof that aliens are out there," I whisper yelled.

"I wouldn't call that proof. You might have accidentally intercepted some walkie talkies from a nearby golf course," He countered.

"There aren't any golf courses nearby!"

"That could explain why it was so faint."

He had me there. Since I couldn't tell what they were saying, I couldn't prove or disprove his theory. If I was going to convince him, I'd have to amplify the audio until you could actually hear something. As I paused to think, the bell rang.

"You'll see, tonight, I'm going to edit the video so you'll clearly be able to hear the aliens," I promised.

"Sure, and when you realize it's a pizza commercial, let me know what special they're running," He laughed.

He won't be laughing when I'm on the news telling the world about how I made first contact with an alien race, or when I get a Nobel peace prize for my radio experiment. My video kept getting hits all day. I was up to 55 notes by the time my last period started. Some of the bigger alien blogs were reblogging, saying I was on to something. I even had a few messages in my inbox about how cool it was, and a few haters, but I'm gonna be the one who gets the last laugh.

As soon as the bell rang, I took off toward home, practically running down the street. I don't live too far from school, so I made it about halfway before having to stop running. I'm not fit enough to run all the way without having some sort of attack. I snuck past the nanny once I got through the door, he won't follow me, and besides, he won't enter my room without warning me first. Homework was going to have to wait, this is the most important thing I've ever done in my entire life.

Running over to my desk, I booted up my computer and turned on the radio, ready to make history. Once my computer was ready, I started turning the knob, tuning the radio to listen to space noise. As I approached the frequency that I'd had it on yesterday, I began to hear something much louder this time.

"M4, Com- -n M4," A voice came, although a few bits and pieces got cut off.

My heart felt like it stopped. My ears were ringing, and my vision was starting to go blurry. This is insane. I can hear them reasonably clearly, and I can understand them! Quickly, I reached to start the stream, but then I paused. Wait, what if some of the viewers report me? FBI agents could be busting through my door any second after I start. They could steal my radio, delete my account, wipe me off the face of the Earth, and no one would know I even existed. I'd be another government cover-up like Amelia Earhart, but I still have to document this.

Instead of starting a stream, I chose to just hit record.

"Hey guys, I think I'm onto something here. That noise we heard yesterday is way louder, now I can hear them! They're looking for someone! This is a two-way radio, so I'm going to try to make contact, wish me luck!"

It took me a minute to get the microphone for the radio working. Once I had it, I took a minute to catch my breath

41

before pressing the button.

"Come in, M4."

"Hello, can you hear me?" I said as slowly and clearly as I could.

There was a pause on the other end, but then the voice returned.

"Hello there. With whom am I speaking?"

"My name's Nikki, Earthling, African American, 16 years of age."

"Hello, I am JUL13T. I've been looking for a friend of mine, and we think she might have crash-landed on your planet," The alien explained.

JUL13T, to me, that looked kind of like Juliet, but I don't think that was the intention. The letters and numbers probably stood for something, and any likeness to a real name was probably just a coincidence.

"Can you tell me about your friend?" I asked.

"Yes, her name is M4T1LD4. She's Malacian by birth, but her alliance is with The Rebellion. About 17 years ago, she went missing in action, and we believe she may have sought refuge on your planet," She replied.

M4T1LD4? Call me crazy, but that kind of looks like Matilda. Now that I think about it, it was about 17 years ago when Galileo's mom "immigrated." Could she be the one they're looking for? I'm not sure, but you never know.

"I think I might know her, but she's taken on an Earth name and adopted a life here."

"That sounds like her. She's excellent at adapting. Could you take us to her?"

"Yeah, totally, but how could you find me? Can you lock in on my location or something?"

42

"Of course and we already have. It won't take us long to get there, so I suggest you prepare for our arrival. If you're right about this, you'll be doing The Rebellion a great service," Juliet said.

"Got it, I'll clear a space for you in the backyard."

"See you soon, Nikki."

"Same to you, over and out."

"Over and out."

Then the radio went back to its usual white noise, totally unchanged, but to me it felt like the world would never be the same. This is bigger than me. These aliens are rebels, helping them might pit Earth against whatever they're rebelling from. I've got to handle this very carefully, no one else can know about this, not even my family. I turned off the camera. There's no way I'm going to post this anytime soon. Besides, I've got to get working on making a space in the back yard and calling Galileo. The phone was already ringing as I slipped out the backdoor.

"What is it, Nikki? Is Papa Johns having a two for one special or something?"

"Bigger than that! I need you to come over right now. This may sound crazy, but I really got something this time! There are some aliens coming, and I think they're looking for your mom," I explained, pulling my younger sibling's playground toward the fence.

"Why would they be looking for my mom, and what do you mean they're coming?"

"They're coming to my house. I'll explain everything when you get over here, so hurry up," I commanded.

It was starting to get dark, my family will probably be asleep by the time they get here.

"Alright, I'm on my way, but I'm stopping to get some pizza

and sodas. All this talking about pizza has made me hungry, and when they don't show up, we'll need something to occupy our time while you make me stay outside," He groaned.

"Whatever, just hurry, and get half Hawaiian."

"Gross, but okay."

I usually sign off with something, but this time I was too focused on cleaning to remember. I just ended the call without a second thought, putting my phone back in my pocket. I wasn't able to clear a massive space for them to land due to this big tree in the middle of our yard, but I still managed to make a substantial area. Hopefully, they'll manage to land. When Galileo showed up with the pizza, it was pitch black, and I was getting some chairs out for us to sit down. He had in his hands one large pizza and two two liters.

"Alright, have the aliens shown, and I just can't see them, or have they not shown up yet?" He joked.

"They haven't come yet, but they'll be here soon."

"Right," He groaned, sitting down in one of the chairs and passing me one of the two liters.

As we sat waiting, we ate pizza and chugged soda like two wild animals, well two wild teenagers. We burned through the pizza like we hadn't eaten in years, then we got to work on the two liters, taking big gulps in between our talking. I explained to him what had happened and what the aliens had said. He looked at me skeptically, but I was confident in what I'd found.

My family had already gone to sleep, so we had to make sure we weren't loud enough to wake any of them up. Quietly, we talked about all sorts of things from the stars to the weather to politics. After about an hour, when Galileo was starting to drift off, I noticed something moving in the sky. It blended into the sky, but I could clearly see it's curvature if I looked closely and followed it across the horizon. I grabbed Galileo's arm and shook it violently, stirring him from his near slumber.

"What? What?!" He snapped.

"Look, do you see that?" I asked, pointing to the object.

"See what?"

"That thing. It's getting closer. Maybe it's them!" I whisper screamed in excitement.

As the object got closer and closer, it changed its angle so that it's back half was lower than its front. Once it was about 30 feet up, it slowly started to change until I could clearly see it. There was no doubt it was a spacecraft. It's slick, chrome design looked nothing like anything we have on Earth, and there's no way any country has managed to master cloaking at that level. Even the way it lowered seemed out of this world, it was so steady, like it wasn't even affected by landing, and it was utterly silent. There was a gust of wind blowing against my face, but that was the only thing it was giving off.

"What is that?" Galileo asked, his eyes popping out of his skull.

"It's the aliens. We did it; they're here! Make yourself presentable star boy so we can really welcome them," I replied.

A door appeared and opened on the side of the craft, a large ramp extending out from the bottom until it reached the ground. Three very human-looking beings stepped out onto the ramp. At the front was a tall black woman with a buzz cut wearing a silver outfit that reflected all the colors that came from the ship. Behind her was a short, Asian looking man with a third eye, wearing a sleek green outfit. Next to him was a tall man that looked like a giant boulder. He had only one eye, and his skin had kind of a rough appearance to it. His clothes were bright red and looked like they were having a hard time containing

45

him.

"Allow me to the be first to welcome you all to Earth. You must be JUL13T, I'm Nikki." I said, taking her hand and shaking it.

"Hello, Nikki. May I ask who that other one is?" Juliet asked, pointing to Galileo, who was currently staring and holding his mouth open.

"That is Galileo. He is the son of the woman that I suspect you're looking for."

She looked at me thoughtfully, pursing her lips.

"M4 did not have a child."

"Oh well, maybe she had him after coming to Earth?" I suggested.

"Maybe," she replied.

"L14NG, BR16S, stay, and watch the ship. If it really is M4, I'll radio for you," She commanded.

The two men nodded and went back inside the ship, leaving the three of us alone outside.

"Lead me to M4," Juliet demanded.

"Sure thing, if you would just follow me, it's just a short walk," I explained.

Galileo was still frozen in shock, so I had to pull him with me at first. Once he snapped out of it, he was staring at the alien in front of him and whispering to me.

"This is crazy! My mom isn't the one they're looking for. When they find out, they'll kill us."

"Don't be so pessimistic. Maybe they'll realize it was an honest mistake and move on. Think about it this way; if it is your mom, we might be giving her back to her old friends."

If I'm being sincere, I knew he was right. These people seemed like they were into some shady stuff, they might be the type to bust your kneecaps before launching you out a trash shoot into space. Even though I said it so confidently, I was having to convince myself that everything was going to be okay.

Since it was so late out, we didn't pass very many people on the way, and the ones we did mostly just kept walking. One man, though, was a bit more curious.

"Hey, lady. Why're you dressed like you just got out of a sci-fi convention?" He teased.

"What do you-" Juliet began, but I quickly cut her off.

"We're taking her Halloween costume for a test drive," I lied.

"In November?"

"Yup, you always want to be prepared, am I right?"

The man didn't seem completely satisfied with my answer, but he left it at that and kept walking. It wasn't long after that when we made it to Galileo's house. I turned to Juliet and presented the home with a showy flick of my arms.

"Here is where I believe your friend has been living," I explained.

"What a small and primitive shelter. If she's been living here, I really hope she's alright," Juliet muttered.

"Here follow me," Galileo said, leading her inside.

We could hear the water running in the kitchen, so we figured Matilda was in there. Before we could go inside Galileo, pulled me aside.

"If this all goes south and gets us killed, I want you to know it was all your fault."

"I know, and I take full responsibility," I replied.

Finishing up our little meeting, we gestured for Juliet to follow us. Matilda was standing at the sink, doing dishes with her back turned to us. She was drying a glass at the moment, turning a rag around inside of it to get the last bit of water.

47

"Hey honey, how was your time at N-" She turned around to address who she thought was only her son, but when she looked at the three of us, her eyes went wide.

The cup in her hand fell to the ground, shattering into tons of tiny splinters.

"JUL?" She spoke, her voice shaky.

"M4!" Juliet yelled, running over and jumping into Matilda's open arms, embracing her as if she were hugging a lost loved one.

6

Chapter 6

Now, here is something I never thought I'd see. There's an alien standing in my house, hugging my mother, who's hugging her back. I couldn't think of anything to say, this was all so overwhelming. Nikki was right, my mother really is an Alien. She didn't just immigrate from another country, and her little idiosyncrasies were due to her being from another planet. It was all too much to process, my head was spinning, and I almost fell, but I grabbed the wall to steady myself. The female alien, whose name I think was Juliet, pulled a little device out of her pocket and held it up to her mouth.

"It's her! It's really her, we found her. Bring the ship, it's time to take M4 home," She yelled excitedly into the little device.

My mom pulled away from her, keeping her hands on her shoulders.

"I can't believe you found me. I thought I was never going to see you all again. I've been trying so hard, but their technology is too primitive for me to work with," Mom explained.

"We searched several galaxies. Everyone told us it was

pointless, but I knew you were still out there! The spirit of The Rebellion lives on!" Juliet replied, giving mom another hug.

As they hugged, mom looked over at me, her face suddenly changing to big a smile. She pulled away from her alien friend and turned her around to face me.

"JUL, this is my son Galileo. I've wanted to introduce you two for a long time," She said, gesturing for me to come forward.

Juliet hurriedly moved forward, taking my hand in both of hers. With a huge smile, she shook it in one of the firmest handshakes I've ever experienced.

"It's so nice to meet you, Galileo. My name's JUL13T, your mother and I have been friends for decades and war partners for even longer. She's the patron saint of The Rebellion, a hero throughout the galaxy, liberator of the people. You've got one hell of a legacy to live up to," She joked.

"I don't know if I'd say all that," My mom laughed.

The two of them were acting like everything was great, like everything was normal, but it wasn't. My world has just been turned upside down, and nobody's helping me reorient myself. I still haven't been able to get a single word in.

"So, who's the dad M4? Did you find a nice little Earthling to settle down with?" Juliet teased."

That's not important right now. I've got so many questions for you."

"I'll answer anything you want once we get on the ship, then I've got some for you. I'm dying to know what happened to you."

"Me too," Nikki interrupted.

Just about everyone had forgotten she was there, so when she spoke, they jumped a little. Mom's face totally changed when she realized what all Nikki had heard.

"Nikki, sweetie, you don't need to get caught up in all of this. You've already done enough to help, and I can't tell you how grateful I am, but you need to go home. Getting involved with all of this could put you in danger, and you've got such a bright future here on Earth. I don't want you to lose that," Mom said, all motherly like.

"Come on, Ms. M! This is everything I've ever dreamed of! Please, just give me a chance to see space, and whatever it is you're involved in so I can make my own decision. Please don't make this decision for me. Maybe I'll want to join your cause if I actually get a chance to see it," Nikki protested.

Mom's face softened, a smile coming to her lips.

"Years ago, I threw away my future for the cause that I believed in. I was ready to do anything it took to bring to life the reality that I wanted for my people. How can I stifle your enthusiasm when I did the same thing?"

Nikki jumped around with joy, dancing like she'd just won some sort of lottery. Mom and Juliet laughed, joining in her little dance.

"What about me? Is anyone going to give me a choice? I mean, maybe I like it here, maybe I want to stay on Earth, did you think about that?" I snapped.

The three of them stopped dancing, looking at me like I'd just killed a puppy in front of them. I may have ruined their moment, but this is a real issue. How can they just expect me to accept all of this and go along with it? My entire life may have been a lie, but that doesn't mean I'm ready to throw it away and embrace the truth. Before either of the others could speak, mom stepped forward and placed her hand on my shoulder. She led me toward the living room, gesturing for the two of them to stay put. We plopped down on the couch, facing each other. Her hands were on her knees, and she had a very concerned look on her face like she was scared I'd break with words too harsh.

"I'm sure you have some questions," She began.

"How could I not?" I interrupted.

"Well, ask away. Ask as many questions as you want, then you can decide whether or not you want to accept it," She explained.

"Alright, rapid-fire. Are you my real mother?"

"Yes, I gave birth to you after 5 months of pregnancy."

"Why did you never tell me you weren't human?"

"I never knew how to address it. I thought it would make life here harder for you."

"What is your real name?"

"M4T1LD4."

"Where are you from?"

"Malacia. The 6th planet in the Ecto system of the Blue Quasar galaxy."

"How did you get here?"

"An escape pod."

"What were you running from?"

"A horrible government that I was leading the fight against."

"Was my father human?""No."

"Who was he?"

"I can't tell you. It would put you in danger."

Hearing all these answers just kept driving home how crazy this all was. I was having a hard time dealing with it. I wanted it all to be a dream, but I knew it wasn't. My life has just been turned upside down, flipped inside out, then reflected across a jagged mirror.

"Alright, I believe you, but I don't want to give up my life here."

"I understand. I've still got work to do, so I definitely have to go back, but you don't. If you want, you can come with us and see everything then decide what you want to do," She offered.

"Alright, but if I say I want to stay here. Promise you won't fight me about it, and you'll come visit sometimes when I ask you to," I replied.

"I promise. Once I'm done, and everything is safe, if you decide to stay here, I'll come back."

She was looking at me with such a genuine and loving expression, it was bringing tears to my eyes. All I could think to do was give her a big hug, squeezing her as tightly as I could. She hugged me right back, her tears falling into my hair.

"I love you," She whispered.

"I love you too. Even if you are an alien," I whispered back.

For a moment, we just stayed there, sharing a moment, but I finally pulled away, wiping the tears from my eyes. Now I was ready to see the world that my mom left behind. When we walked back into the kitchen, the two men from before were now standing next to Juliet. Mom squealed with joy upon seeing them.

"L14! BR1!" She yelled, running up and hugging the two of them.

They seemed super excited to see her, much like how Juliet was a few minutes before.

"We brought your ship," The Asian looking man, L14, said.

"Starhopper?" My mom shrieked excitedly.

The two men nodded, leading all of us out the back door. The space ship from before was now parked in our backyard, it's bright silver exterior reflecting all the color lights as we approached it. We could see our reflections, although slightly distorted, looking back at us. Mom ran up and placed her hands on the side, staring at it like a small child. She looked so happy to see it; she even rubbed her face up against it, nuzzling it lovingly.

"After the fight at the omega quasar, everyone gave up on you, except us. We took your ship and immediately started looking for you." The big rock looking alien explained.

Hearing this, mom's face changed; she straightened up and headed toward the side of the ship. Pressing a panel on the side, the door from before appeared, the same ramp extending out towards her.

"Speaking of, let's get going, I need to know the state of The Rebellion," She said as she climbed up the ramp.

The three aliens nodded, following behind her like well-trained soldiers. Nikki and I followed soon after. She was texting as she walked, probably making up some lie to her babysitter. Since her parents are on that trip, they won't notice that she's not home, and her babysitter won't worry if he thinks she's accounted for.

Inside the ship was even more futuristic looking than the outside. The door took us right into a big room with several chairs that I guessed was the cockpit. At the very front was a chair right in front of a large board full of buttons and switches. There were screens everywhere displaying different numbers and diagrams. Mom walked right up to the front and sat in the head seat. The others followed behind her, taking the three seats closest to her, while Nikki and I had to sit in the ones farthest in the back. She placed her hand on one of the screens, the ship reacting with a low hum. Suddenly, we could feel the ship lifting slightly off the ground. Mom hit another big red button before grabbing the throttle lever to her right.

"Hang on kids, this baby can travel at ten thousand times the speed of light. We're about to make the jump out of Earth's atmosphere," She warned.

Two odd-looking straps popped out of our chairs and wrapped around us. They magnetized in the center of my chest, flashing a bright blue where the two pieces met. Nikki looked like she was having the time of her life, taking pictures of the interior with her phone as mom angled the ship upward.

"Here we go!" She yelled, pushing the throttle nearly all the way to the metal.

The ship lurched forward, the force pushing me against the seat so hard my head whipped back. Mom and the other aliens didn't seem affected, they just stared straight ahead with big smiles on their faces.

I forced my head to turn and look at Nikki, who was in a similar predicament as me. Her face was blown backward, her mouth hanging open and her neck leaning back. We looked like two riders on a rollercoaster that had a drop we weren't expecting, while the aliens looked like there was maybe a slight breeze.

Just as quickly as we took off, we stopped. Outside the front window, I could see Neptune, it's beautiful blue expanse seeming to look back at me. We were still moving, but much slower, kind of like we were just drifting along. Mom spun her chair around, pushing the spot where the two straps met, causing it to glow blue again and release, going back into the chair. The other aliens did the same, but when I tried, I think I missed it because it took me a few tries.

"So, where should we be heading?" Mom asked.

"Head to Ipo in sector three," L14 replied.

"Why not Roran?"

"Our base on Roran was abandoned after you disappeared, those of us who were still on your side headed to Ipo," Juliet explained.

"What do you mean by that?" Mom asked, punching in some numbers.

This time, when the ship took off, the force didn't push me against the chair. I could still move and walk around, but I could tell we were again moving really fast. Maybe we just weren't moving as fast as before. Mom turned around once the ship was in autopilot, crossing her arms and legs with a confused look on her face.

"Well, when you disappeared, there were many theories about what happened to you. The Rebellion was split into factions, depending on what theory they believed. Each one then diverged and either created a new base or chose to go back to their lives in the The Senatee." Juliet explained.

"And what were these theories?"

"Well, one was that you had died," L14 answered.

"Another was that you were a double agent who orchestrated the entire thing to cripple The Rebellion and return to life in The Senate," BR1 added.

"Then there were those of us who believed you survived and had managed to somehow escape," Juliet finished.

Mom nodded as they spoke, her finger placed under her chin thoughtfully. When she heard the one BR1 suggested, her eye twitched.

"So, what did happen?" Nikki asked from the back.

The aliens looked back at her, then to mom expectantly. She smiled and leaned back in her chair.

"Well get ready you all, this is going to be the story of a lifetime," She began. "Years ago, at the Omega quasar, everything seemed to be going incredibly. AL1TH1US had taken the bait and was leading the battle from his place in his imperial destroyer. Everything was in place, if we were able to win, we'd be able to cripple The Senate and take over, and it seemed like we were going to do it. We had them outnumbered and were closing in on the destroyer. I was leading from my place in The Rebellion's war machine, when all of a sudden, a bright light appeared. A huge beam shot from the destroyer, smashing through the war machine and tossing me and all other members of the crew out into space. My life support system immediately kicked in, surrounding my head in an oxygen bubble. As I checked to make sure my system was fully functional, I noticed all the others floating through space with their own oxygen bubbles on. I was the only one among them that had a functioning jet propulsion system, so I activated it and tried to bring them to safety, but a second beam of light surrounded me. A tractor beam pulled me towards the head of the destroyer, and no matter how hard I tried, I couldn't get out of its grasp. As soon as I was inside, they locked me up. For months I was tortured, as AL1TH1US went and destroyed hundreds of Rebellion ships on his way back to Malacia. One day, he was sloppy, however, and I managed to escape and steal an escape pod. I drove it as fast as it could go as far away as possible until I crash-landed on Earth when the pod ran out of fuel," She explained.

Everyone on the ship was sitting on the edges of their seats. I was able to get the gist of it all, but there were some things I didn't really understand, mostly the war jargon. A lot of those words didn't mean anything to me, but clearly, it meant something to the aliens because they had their mouths open in shock.

"What happened after that?" Nikki asked.

"I abandoned the ship and took off looking for shelter until I could figure out what to do. There was no way I'd be getting the ship back since the intelligent life on the planet would be coming for it, so I was stuck hiding out in an abandoned house outside a small town. For the first few weeks, I tried to fashion some crude communication equipment using the materials inside, but I wasn't able to make much headway, and I was getting ridiculously hungry. Leaving my shelter, I went looking for something edible, which took a little bit of trial and error. Apparently, I wasn't sneaky enough, because a group of humans came to help me. They said they were from the Way Of LIfe Synagogue in town and that their members had raised a lot of money to help me get on my feet. The rest is history from there, I got a job, had Galileo, fixed up the house, and did my best to try to adapt to my new life on Earth."

"I'm so sorry, M4. We tried to get you back, but the destroyer took out too many of our ships, we couldn't even get within a thousand meters. As soon as we could, we took your ship and went looking for you, but we couldn't tell where to start. AL1TH1US returned to Malacia without you, and nobody knew where you went and," Juliet said, her eyes downcast.

"It's ok. I made it through. Life on Earth wasn't too bad. I met some very nice people and learned a lot about their culture. Plus, I was able to raise my son in a safe environment."

"But you shouldn't have had to. You should have been there with us, why didn't you try to come back to us? You could have put in the coordinates for our base," L14NG, questioned.

"The thought crossed my mind, but they'd be able to track the pod from that distance. I would have led them right to you."

"Right, good thinking," L14NG corrected himself.

58

"Thank you. Now enough about me, tell me what our numbers are. I want to know where we're at right now," Mom asked.

Nikki and BR16S had moved to the back and were talking about the ship and how it worked. There was a lot of astronomy stuff involved, and Nikki looked like she was in heaven listening to all of it, taking in what she could.

"Not too good. As of right now, the only members of The Rebellion that are still loyal to you are sitting in this ship. Two minor rebellion groups are still active, but they claim no allegiance to you," Juliet explained.

"Yikes, that's a problem. Do you think we'll be able to get them back on my side?"

"I'm not sure. They're pretty adamant about their beliefs. They were saying that they'd have your head if you ever came back," L14NG added.

"Alright, then our first priority should be to get them back on our side. Once we go to Ipo and restock, we should set a course for their base. There should be plenty of space for all of us to sleep until we get there. How are we on food?" Mom asked.

"We're fine. Just restocked two systems ago," Juliet replied.

"Wonderful. Well, it's been a long day, how about we all settle down for the night?" Mom suggested, standing from her seat and heading toward the back of the cockpit.

"Of course, your room, as well as one spare room, are open."

"Excellent. Nikki, you can have the spare room, Galileo and I can share mine."

"Alright!" Nikki cheered, following Juliet through the door.

Mom placed a hand on my shoulder and followed behind the two of them. The ship was actually massive inside. There was a whole hallway and everything behind the cockpit. Juliet and

Nikki went down one hall, while mom and I went the opposite way. There was only one door down this way. It had a weird-looking logo on it, and mom's alien name was stamped below that. There was a panel on the wall that glowed brightly when she placed her hand on it, the door following suit. It opened a little slowly, probably from the lack of use. Inside, the room was actually pretty big. There was a big bed, a couch, a desk covered in paper and war plans, a chair, a bathroom, and several big windows that allowed us to see space as it whizzed by.

Mom walked over to the couch and pulled the cushion outward, transforming it into a pretty comfy looking bed.

"You can sleep here tonight. It'll be just like we're camping," she explained with a smile.

While I took a moment to test out the bed, mom turned and went toward a closet over to the right. She pulled something out before walking into the bathroom, shutting the door behind her. When she returned, she was wearing a bright blue and silver space suit that sparkled and shone.

"This is so much better," She said, tossing her old clothes toward the corner of the room.

She tossed a second pair of clothes at me, these were bright blue and sparkled just the same as hers.

"Here, I ordered a men's uniform on accident a little while back. You can have it."

"Oh, thanks, but I think I'd like to stick with my earth clothes if that's ok," I replied.

"Alright, pumpkin. Let me get you a pillow and blanket," Mom offered, turning to another small closet.

From there, she produced a small pillow and fluffy looking blanket. She tossed the pillow to me, then spread the blanket out over my body. Mom fell asleep before I had even gotten comfortable. Apparently, her bed was perfect to put her right to sleep. I'm not saying the bed I was on wasn't pleasant, it just didn't feel like home. It was like lying in a stranger's bed, in a strange place, and I just couldn't relax. My mind was still reeling from everything that had happened today. In a matter of less than twenty-four hours, my entire life had been turned on its head and flipped inside out. I couldn't think I couldn't sleep, all I could do was stare up at the ceiling. Eventually, I drifted off when I had grown too tired to keep my eyes open.

7

Chapter 7

I was sleeping just fine when a horrific sounding alarm woke me up. My mind was still holding on to the remnants of my sleep as I slowly lifted my head. Through the tired haze, I was able to see my mother dash out of the room.

Everything on the ship looked terrifying bathed in the red light of the warning alarms. Nikki came out of her room, rubbing her eyes as I was heading toward the front. "What's going on?" She mumbled, yawning in the middle.

"I don't know, whatever it is, it's got mom spooked," I replied, taking her hand and leading her toward the cockpit.

There were all sorts of lights flashing and warning messages being displayed on the control panel. Mom was at the front next to the other aliens frantically reading the lines of text while pressing buttons.

"How long have they been following us?" She asked.

"Since we passed Iroh. They're closing in on us now," Juliet replied.

"Do we have a visual?"

"On screen now," L14 called from his place in his chair.

At the front of the ship, a big hologram appeared, showing our ship in front being chased by a much larger one. It was probably four times the size of ours, and from the looks of it, it was equipped for battle. There were strange symbols all over the side, which I guessed were to show their alliance to something.

"I don't recognize those symbols," Mom admitted.

"You wouldn't, that's one of the factions. The Fallen, they're the ones that believe you betrayed The Rebellion," L14 explained.

"We can try and outrun them," BR1 suggested.

A moment later, the ship creaked and lurched to the side. According to the hologram, two arms had sprouted out of the other vessel and grabbed onto us.

"Any other day, I'd say yes, but two things are stopping us. One, if we take off now or try to stop, those arms will rip the sides off my ship, and we can't afford to take that kind of damage right now. Two, running will just make me look even more guilty. We have to face them head-on if we're going to get them back on our side," Mom explained.

She was standing there at the front of the ship with her arms crossed, back straight, and a bold, determined look on her face. At that moment, she looked every bit like a leader of an interstellar rebellion. The sweet single mother that worked at the convenience store was no more, replaced by a hardened alien badass.

"They're attempting to board."

"Unlock the roof hatch, let them in," my mom commanded.

Juliet pressed a button, causing a latch somewhere to click. Soon after, the sound of several feet hitting the roof resonated through the cockpit. The hatch opened and several people dressed in strange, futuristic-looking space suits hopped down into our ship. Each one had a gun, or at least I assumed they were guns, that glowed and blinked, unlike anything we had on Earth. Everyone put their hands up, showing them that we weren't looking to fight. The last person to jump down was a rough-looking man with a cape and horns added to his suit. He scanned the room, looking at all of us with disgust.

"JUL, BR1, and L14, you are all under arrest for conspiring against The Fallen. Your ship and it's passengers will be taken for inspection, you three will be getting a trial at an undisclosed-"

"Seriously, M0RW1N? All this legal talk, we can't even get a hello?" Mom interrupted, spinning around in her chair, revealing herself to the intruders.

They all stepped back in shock, especially the man with the horns. You'd think they'd seen a ghost or the devil himself with how badly they were quivering. Shaking off the shock, he grit his teeth at her.

"You have some nerve coming around here M4! After what you did to The Rebellion, I should shoot you where you stand," he threatened.

"If you're so sure I've done something wrong, how about putting me on trial? I deserve the right to defend myself, do I not?" Mom replied smugly.

"We don't need a trial, I'd be more than happy to launch your sorry ass out into space right now!"

"But you won't, we're civilized people, and besides, doesn't everyone want to know what really happened?" Mom rebuked.

"We don't want to hear your lies!"

"Even so, wouldn't your people be pissed if they found out you just killed me? You're robbing your people of closure. I

64

think they'd rather try me and have me publicly executed rather than you launching me," Mom added.

I was utterly speechless watching the exchange. This man had a gun to her face, and Mom was talking without the slightest hint of fear in her voice. Apparently, she was saying all the right things because the man appeared to be backing off.

"Whatever, arrest her, I'll tell the council we're bringing her in. They'll get the trial ready," he ordered, putting his gun away.

Two soldiers ran over and handcuffed mom using these weird, metal, and laser looking cuffs. The rest of us were put into regular cuffs that locked our hands behind our backs. They herded us like cattle toward a ladder that someone from the other ship tossed down. It was kind of hard to climb with just our legs, but we managed. Those big robotic arms pulled us inside the larger ship; once there, the men led us toward a holding cell. At first, the cell seemed insanely large, perfect for all of us to stay in. There was a glass wall in the front, but other than that, everything was bleak and white.

Everyone except mom was pushed to the right; once we were all in place, a wall of lasers appeared from the floor, separating us.

"And this is for?" My mother asked, looking at the lasers.

"To make sure you all don't try any funny business," the man from before replied.

Mom shrugged her shoulders and sat down crisscrossed.

"Fine by me."

Juliet moved to stand between the man from before and us. Even through the bars, you could tell she made him a bit nervous. The other soldiers kept their guns trained on her, even though she couldn't get to them.

"I always knew you didn't have it in you," she hissed.

"Didn't have it in me? Just because I didn't sell my heart and soul to this woman like you three did means I didn't have it? The three of you were so blindsided that you couldn't see the writing on the wall! She betrayed us, and when we get back to the city, the truth will come out. Then, she'll hang for the lives of everyone who died at the foot of her lies," The man yelled back at her.

I could see a vein popping out on the side of his head. He's obviously very passionate about this, maybe he knows something I don't? Now, that's something I hadn't thought of. What if it turns out that my mother really did betray all these people? I don't think she would, but lately, I'm not sure if I even know her.

When I peeked at her out of the corner of my eye, mom was looking at M0W with the most pained expression I've ever seen on her face. I wanted to believe that the look was genuine, but even crocodile tears can trick an outsider.

"Viva La Revolution!" Nikki yelled, kicking the bars out of nowhere, surprising everyone.

Welp, she's dead. Love you, Nikki, but I'm sure you've just signed your own death warrant. They're going to kill her to make an example for the rest of us, and there's nothing I can do about that. As the shock subsided, M0RW1N started laughing, a deep rumbling sound that reverberated throughout our tiny cell.

"That's the same kind of energy I had when I first joined The Rebellion. Good to know the spirit is still alive. Maybe once we get back to the city, we can work on recruiting you. I'm sure you'd do better with us than these dirty traitors," M0RW1N explained, turning away from us to head somewhere else, his cape flapping around behind him.

"Never! My loyalty is with Matilda! You will never get me to the dark side- and he's gone," Nikki sighed.

Mom and the other aliens moved closer to her, or at least as close as mom could with the lasers, praising her for her bravery."

That was awesome, Nikki! If I didn't have to take you back home, I'd recruit you right here."

"Really?! You'd want me for The Rebellion?"

"Of course! You've got real moxie kiddo, and your loyalty is indispensable. It would be an honor having you."

"That's right, I'd be happy to have you as my assistant platoon leader," Juliet added.

"As if! She'd want to be in mechanics with me," BR16S argued.

"No way! She's too smart for that, she'd be a strategist like me," L14NG insisted.

"You're all wrong, she'd be on the field with me. I'd make her my honorary Colonel," Mom laughed.

They were sitting there, laughing like we weren't currently sitting in a cell in handcuffs on a strange spaceship hurtling toward an entire city of people who were all probably sharpening the guillotine so they could chop my mom's head off. The insanity of it all could have knocked me to the ground if I weren't leaning up against the cell wall.

"Am I the only sane one here?" I interrupted.

Everyone turned to look at me like I had just run over their parade. If I'm honest, I don't think I'm the one acting crazy here.

"What's wrong, kiddo?" BR16S asked, moving towards me to try and be comforting.

"Look, don't take this the wrong way, but it seems to me like I'm the only here who's taking this whole thing seriously. Did he not just get through saying that he and everyone on the planet we're on the way to wants my mom dead, and we're just supposed to act like everything is fine?" I explained.

They all gave me these sweet knowing looks, like what you'd give to a little kid that fell and hurt its knee. It was infuriating, being treated like a child.

"Look, baby, this isn't our first rodeo. Do you know how many times I've been on the chopping block? More than I could ever hope to count. I was nervous the first time, yes, but at this point, I'm used to it," Mom replied, looking at me sweetly through the lasers.

She got a little bit too close, causing a tiny little jolt to pop out and hit her cheek.

The rest of the trip was pretty uneventful. In five minutes, we weren't actually able to get into anything. Several sets of footsteps approached our cell right after the ship lurched a bit as it docked. The tiny hallway was soon filled with soldiers that all had their guns on us. There were more soldiers on mom's side than on ours, a bit weird when you think about how there are five times as many people on this side than that one, but whatever that's their decision.

There was a second alien all decked out in armor this time. It was a woman, an adult, with one of the stoniest gazes I've ever seen. Her outfit didn't have horns or anything, but she was still dressed in one hell of an intimidating outfit. I could see my reflection in every piece of metal with the slightest of blue tints. It was unlike any metal I'd seen on Earth.

"Alright prisoners, you are all witnesses to M4T1LD4's war crimes and will be treated as such. When I open this cell door, you will follow me to the courtroom where your files will be brought up for use during the trial. I would suggest you cooperate. Right now, none of you are off the hook, and depending on the results of the trial, M4 might not be the only one getting executed," she explained.

"I plead the fifth!" Nikki yelled.

"The fifth what?" Juliet asked.

"It means I don't have to say anything to them."

"I would suggest doing so, otherwise, the council won't be so lenient with your punishment," The female alien interrupted.

The glass walls lifted and the aliens moved in on us. They had their guns pointed at our backs; some went so far as to press their barrels against us. It was terrifying having a weapon touching me, but what was more frightening was seeing the soldiers take my mother away. She was led down one hall while the rest of us were led down another. All I got was one last worried glimpse before she was gone.

The five of us were lead to a small white room with an androgynous alien sitting at what I assumed was a computer. It was more like a hologram screen that they pressed buttons on. From our side, we couldn't see anything, but from her side, it looked like whatever it was she was using it for. Each one of us was called up.

"State your name and species," The alien commanded.

"JUL13T, Vaad."

The alien typed a few things onto the pad before gesturing for her to take a step forward.

"Next."

"L14NG, Chotieth."

"Next."

"BR16S, Moltais."

"Next."

Nikki went up before me, that same rebellious look on her face. This is precisely what she's been dreaming of for years, I bet she's having the time of her life.

"Nikki, Human."

The alien stopped typing and looked at her.

"What? Please spell that."

"N I K K I, H U M A N, Nikki, Human."

"And what is your planet of origin?"

"Earth, E A R T H."

After a bit more typing, the alien called for me.

"You aren't going to be a pain like the last one, are you?" They groaned.

"I hope not. My name's Galileo, G A L I L E O, and I'm not sure what species I am."

"What do you mean you don't know?!"

"His mother is Vaad, but we don't know what species his father is," Juliet spoke up.

"For now, I'll just put Vaad/Undetermined." The alien replied.

I was pushed back into the group right as a door opened in front of us, we were led into a vast room that resembled something out of the Vatican. The ceiling rose for what seemed like forever, amplifying the shouts of the hundreds of people sitting around the stands. There was a long table at which sat six aliens, all looking down at my mother. Behind them was a huge glass window that opened up to the expanse of space. Every now and then, a part of the base swung by.

In front of said table was a pit, in the middle of said pit was a tiny little platform that my mother was standing on. She looked up at those aliens with a determined look in her eyes, ready to take their scrutiny. The five of us were lead to a larger platform where four other aliens with weapons were standing. Once we were all on, a rail appeared behind us, and the platform moved so that it was to the right and behind the one mom was on.

With everything in place, the alien at the head of the table pounded his gavel, silencing the rambunctious crowd.

"Today, we are here to determine the fate of our former leader, a traitor to The Rebellion, and a murderer!" He yelled.

The alien to his right, which I think was female, stood up next.

"M4T1LD4, you have chosen to represent yourself, is that correct?" She asked.

"Yes, I don't need anyone's help to prove my innocence."

"A foolish decision really," One of the aliens on the left chimed in.

The alien at the front banged his gavel once again.

"Then let the trial commence. P3TR4, you may begin."

The female alien from before stepped forward, allowing me to get a better look at her. She looked pretty close to human, but a lot of the skin around her neck was scaly, and her pupils were slanted. When she looked down at my mother, her eyes shot daggers. Just seeing it was enough to make me shiver, and I wasn't even the target!

In front of her was a glowing pad, like the one the alien who took our information had. She scrolled up and down, checking a few things before beginning.

"M4T1LD4, you were born on Malacia to the general G0RD4N correct?"

"Yes."

"You were raised to be the perfect soldier for AL1TH1US's army, correct?"

"Yes, as soon as I could stand, I was trained to fight. While children my age were reading books, I was studying war plans."

"After your father's death, you acted as general for 20 solar years, correct?"

"Yes, and I never kept that a secret from The Rebellion."

"Indeed. As general, you had to be in close contact with AL1TH1US, I mean that's part of being a general."

"Up until I made my allegiance to The Rebellion public."

"Interesting. So you just want us to trust that you cut off all communication? What's to say you didn't keep something on you that he could have tracked?"

"I can't exactly prove that untrue, but I will say I did remove all my communication to The Senate from my person."

I wasn't sure where this was going exactly, and that terrified me. Although, even if I did know, I don't think that would make much of a difference.

"Right. At the battle of the Omega Quasar, you were the only one who was pulled into the destroyer, why was that?"

"Probably because I'm the leader. It would have been more effective for him to present me defeated to the people, although it wouldn't have hurt to present all of us."

"Exactly! Why would AL1TH1Us only take you into custody when he could have had you and the majority of your officers? It would have made a bigger impact if he presented all of you, wouldn't it?"

Mom didn't have anything to say about that. She made a thoughtful face but didn't say anything in return.

"A little shady, huh? Who's to say you hadn't told AL1TH1US about our planned attack to use it as an excuse to return to his side? While your officers died out in space, you were pulled into his ship and taken to a remote planet where you could live out the rest of your life in secret while the fake rebellion you made crumbled, weren't you?!"Her hands shaking, mom's face twisted into one of pure rage.

"I'd never return to that bastard! He took me into his ship and did horrible things to me. That sick son of a bitch will never have my loyalty."

"Well then, why don't you tell us what happened? Tell us what happened once you were taken aboard his ship, why you didn't return until now."

The council of aliens looked at mom expectantly. From their expressions, I could tell they had no intention of listening but wanted to keep up the air that this was a fair trial.

"Come on, M4," Juliet whispered beside me.

Taking a deep breath, mom began her story.

"I was taken aboard the destroyer where I was immediately restrained. They took me to a room and strapped me down to a chair. They attached all sorts of machines to me and then knocked me out. When I woke up, AL1TH1US was there. He told me I was an idiot for trying to start a rebellion, that what I was doing was nothing more than a riot that would disappear like all the others. Then for the next three months, he came to that room every day, torturing me with those horrible machines while he showed me footage of his ships destroying rebel bases. One day, while the ship was undergoing maintenance, I managed to sneak out and steal an escape pod. I wanted to return to The Rebellion. Still, I didn't know where I could go, and even if I did, I would have led him straight to us, so I drove that thing until it crash-landed on a remote planet I'd never heard of. The intelligent life on that planet stormed the pod, I just barely managed to escape before they took it to be studied. I was left there on a strange world with no way of contacting anyone. The technology there was too primitive to make anything useful, trust me I tried, so I accepted defeat and made a life for myself."

"And how did he find all of those rebel bases? You must have told him because they were a secret to everyone but our own."

"He never told me, but it's possible he had an informant or maybe multiple."

"Oh, he had an informant alright, you! Why else would he have let you 'escape' to a remote planet? Those pods can be tracked, you know."

"By the time they realized I was gone, I was out of range."

"A likely story. You took that escape pod and left to a planet where you knew you wouldn't be found. One with a species that you could hide amongst and reproduce with!"

Mom made a perplexed face at that last part.

"That's right, we know about your son. Found a nice little native to settle down with, huh? Something to distract you from your sins?"

Below me, the floor suddenly split, leaving me standing on a small platform like mom's that floated over until I was just a few feet from her. She looked terrified for the first time during this trial.

"That's not true! I was pregnant with him before I got to Earth. Leave my son out of this!"

"Then who's his father?"

I'd always wanted to know the answer to that question, but this wasn't how I wanted to find out. I looked at mom who looked back at me before turning to her friends. Tears were welling up in her eyes, and she had to put her head down.

"His father is the only man I was in contact with during those three months."

Gasps spread throughout the courtroom as some people started to put it together. Behind us, her friends cried out in horror. Now, mom was full-blown crying, her entire body shaking.

"So you're saying-"

"That's right, ladies and gentlemen! You're looking at the heir to both The Senate and The Rebellion. My darling son Galileo!"

Mom didn't look alright. She was smiling, but she was still crying, it was scary. The female alien that was running the questioning seemed a bit taken aback, but she quickly bounced back.

"Now, one bit of information that you failed to share with The Rebellion was that before your mutiny, you were the popular choice for queen."

Wiping her eyes, mom regained her composure.

"I didn't think it mattered. It wasn't by my choice."

"But that's not to say you didn't like the idea! You had his child, you could have wanted all this from the start."

"I never-"

Suddenly mom stopped talking. She looked to the left then to the right, seemingly fixated on these floating machines aimed at her face. I thought they were just weapons, but mom's reaction suggested they were something else.

"Are you broadcasting this?" She asked.

"Only to our allies, let's continue with the-" Another alien began, but mom interrupted.

"Didn't I teach you anything?! There are eyes everywhere. By now, AL1TH1US has already intercepted the signal and is on his way."

The crowd began to panic. They started to get up to run, but the head alien pounded the table once again.

"This is a secure broadcast being sent to only our most trusted comrades, the only way he could find us is if-"

Through the window, we could all see as a massive spaceship appeared, followed by several smaller ones. The smaller ones descended upon the base, shooting buildings and taking out weapons. Tremors rocked the courtroom, knocking people off their feet, loud crashes filling the empty space. Somewhere I heard something shatter above all the screams. The head aliens panicked, looking back and forth between the people and the incoming armada. They stood up, barely able to maintain their footing with all the tremors.

"Everyone quickly get to your designated emergency zones. Guards protect the people," The female alien yelled.

While everyone was panicking, mom and her friends were fiddling with their restraints. "These things certainly are flashy, but not that functional," Mom quipped. Relaxing her shoulders, she managed to move her arm upward, causing the blue lasers to zap her. Despite the pain, she kept going until the lasers connecting her two arms dissipated. After that, she just had to pull the cuffs off.

When I looked over, mom's friends had already done the same and were helping Nikki out of hers. The guards that had been watching them had left to help with the evacuation. They were too confident in those restraints.

"Come on, baby, we've got to get you guys out of here," Mom said as she landed on my platform.

In a flash, she pulled my restraints off. Before I could protest, she'd picked me up and tossed me over to the side of the pit. The other aliens joined us once Nikki was free.

"Let's get 'em, boys!" Nikki yelled from BR16S's arms.

She was ready to go kick some alien ass, but we were outnumbered, outgunned, and way out of our league. There's no way we can pull this off. I'm about to die out in space, and I won't be able to see Leery's face when I ace his final.

"BR, JUL, and L14 take the kids and get out of here. Starhopper can get you to the nearest system before they can catch you as long as you keep the cloaking device on. I'll distract them until you get there," Mom ordered.

"We can't just leave you, not after what happened," Juliet protested.

"If he catches Galileo, it's all over. Nikki, if I don't make it back, please ask your parents to watch him for me."

"What do you mean if you don't make it? You're the good guy, you've got this," Nikki argued.

"That's sweet, dear, but life isn't always fair. It doesn't matter who's good and who's evil, what matters is who has the power, and right now, that's not us." Mom said, placing a hand on Nikki's shoulder.

Behind us, the large glass window shattered as rubble launched through it. The noises from outside got even louder, and we could feel the wind from the explosions. The screams were chilling, filling me with even more dread.

"Alright, everyone go!" Mom said, taking off out the window. "Come on, kids."

Mom's friends led Nikki and me in the opposite direction of mom, towards where they were keeping Starhopper. They'd put it next to all their other spaceships, which they were using to evacuate. As we got close, Juliet yelled for the ship to turn on, which it did, the lights came on, and the engine roared. The door opened, and we hopped on as quickly as we could.

"I can't let him get our son, I can't let him get our son, I can't let him get our son," Matilda repeated over and over as she ran across the courtyard.

She ignored everything around her, focusing only on gaining the attention of the armada. If they concentrate on her, they won't notice Starhopper escaping. What she was going to do after that, she wasn't sure, but as long as her son and friends made it out safely, she didn't care.

"Hey! Over here, you pompous sack of spacial bullshit!" She yelled, waving her arms around above her head.

It seemed she wasn't high enough up for anyone to see her. With all the chaos, she just disappeared in the crowd; if she was going to get their attention, she was going to have to get higher up. Over to her right, she could see where a building had partially collapsed, creating a sort of ramp she could use. To get there, she'd have to cross a long distance full of people running around like ants in a partially destroyed anthill, but she wasn't worried. Taking a deep breath, she took off, weaving through people, ducking under flailing limbs. The crowd cleared at the edge of the destroyed building, making it easy for Matilda to start her ascent. She had to jump over a few uneven broken pieces, but overall it was an easy climb. When she reached the top, she started flailing her arms once again, screaming even louder. The main ship turned its attention toward her, locking in on her position. A bright light just like the one she remembered from the battle at the Omega Quasar surrounded her, lifting her and a piece of the building she was standing on. A deep whirring sound filled her ears, drowning out the screams.

She's never been one to accept defeat; no matter how bad things look, Matilda was always looking for a way to get out, but now she accepted her fate. If her loss meant her son and friends would be able to escape, then she didn't care. There was no telling what would happen to her, she had no idea what she was going to say what lies to weave, but that didn't matter. A strange sense of euphoria came over her for the first time, but then it faded away when she realized a second beam was being shot out. Her heart nearly burst when she realized that Starhopper was what was being pulled upward.

"Damnit!' Juliet yelled, smashing buttons on the control panel.

The entire cockpit was bathed in a striking red light as countless error messages took over the screens.

"They got M4!" L14NG yelled, his hands on the back of Juliet's chair.

"Yeah, and they've got us too!" Juliet replied, pushing as hard as she could on the throttle.

Behind us, I could hear the engine screaming in protest as it tried it's hardest to break from the tractor beam. For a moment, we stayed still, the thrust from the ship equaling the pull of the beam, but then I heard the engine blow.

"The engine's fucked!" BR16S yelled, coming from the back of the ship with soot all over his face.

"The backup generators've blown, we're losing thrust," L14NG panicked.

The ship started to move back toward the tractor beam, the emergency warnings getting even louder. They were deafening at this point, I had to cover my ears to deal with the pain. Nikki was doing the same, her eyes brimming with tears. A door on the bottom of the other ship opened, and the tractor beam pulled us in. Thick metal tubes attached themselves to the vessel, sneaking their way in. Suddenly, the cockpit started to fill with a white gas that almost looked like dry ice. Above the sirens, I could just barely hear Juliet scream for us not to breathe it in. There wasn't enough time, I'd already taken a few breaths, and everything faded to black.

"No, no, no, no, no!" Matilda shrieked as Starhopper was pulled inside of the warship. Looking up, she realized she was almost there herself, the bright light nearly blinding her. Below her, she could see people still running around on the ground toward the remaining ships while the others were already far off. Even though these people were just calling for her death, Matilda was happy to see them escaping. At one point, they'd been her best friends, her team, her army, no matter what they would always hold a special place in her heart. There was nothing they could ever do to change that.

Next to her, a loud robotic shifting sound could be heard, followed by a whirring sound and a bright green light. When she turned, she realized that the warship had armed its ultimate weapon.

"No! There are still people down there! You'll kill them!" Matilda screamed as loud as she could, knowing it was futile but hoping beyond all hope that someone would hear her and call it off.

Passing through the threshold of the ship, Matilda found herself in a bleak room with the beam at the top. Below her, the doors began to close, the sound of the weapon growing distant. The gap between the doors was just barely a sliver when the gun finally fired. Matilda was only able to see the light leaving the weapon, but she knew what came next. It was such a loud explosion, the room around her shook. The beam above her turned off, dropping her onto the floor, tears fell from her face to the ground, useless and broken. A loud, hissing sound filled the room as the sleeping gas was injected inside.

8

Chapter 8

"His body seems to be reacting well. Goodness! Your mother should have known better than to deny you proper medical care."

My head felt like a tiny explosion was begging to burst through my skull and splatter my brains. The noises around me sounded like I was underwater listening in. When I opened my eyes, a bright light blinded me, a figure appearing in front of it.

"There you are dear, how are you feeling?" A woman asked.

My eyes slowly adjusted to the bright light, revealing a small, sterile room with devices I didn't recognize. The woman was a doctor I assumed based on her clothes, and I was sat in her office. Next to me, a line of several needles sat on a sterile metal tray, each one a different color.

"My head hurts a little," I admitted, rubbing the back of my neck.

The chair squeaked like leather when I went to move my arm, although I doubt it really was leather. There probably aren't cows in space.

"That'll go away in a little while." The doctor said, turning to her tray of needles and grabbing a bright blue one.

When she turned back to me, I caught a glimpse of the nametag on her coat; LUC1ND4. The needle in her hand slowly approached my arm, the tip nearly touching me. Now is such a terrible time to admit that I have a terrible fear of needles. Although I don't think it matters much right now as the needle is already poised to penetrate my arm. The tip goes in, and I tense up, I shut my eyes like the doctors had told me to do in the past, bracing myself for that weird heated feeling as the medicine works its way inside of me. By the time I open my eyes, the doctor has removed the needle and placed it on a separate metal table. The medical assistant that I hadn't noticed before came and took the used needle away.

The next needle was green, I tensed up, but I didn't even feel it. I didn't feel the puncturing of my skin, the feeling of liquid being forced into my flesh. It was like it never happened; there wasn't even a tiny little red spot left on my arm.

"Is something wrong, dear?" LUC1ND4 asked, setting the used needle down and picking up a new one, pink this time.

"Not exactly. It's just that didn't hurt at all."

"Should it have?" The doctor asked, giving me my next shot.

"It did back home," I said, rubbing the spot where the needle had gone in.

It wasn't even sore.

"Really? Goodness, where did your mother take you? It's a miracle you're still alive," She said, shaking her head.

With the last needle on her tray used up, she moved it aside, reaching below her to grab a new plate full of even more colorful medicines. Her assistant came and took the old tray, taking it somewhere to be disposed of.

"Sorry for all of the injections. Normally you'd have gotten these as a baby when you wouldn't have even noticed, but since you've been outside of The Senate, we have to get you caught up on three solar years of immunizations," She explained, injecting me with a purple liquid.

"It's alright. I'd rather be safe," I said, looking toward a window behind me.

I couldn't really tell where I was. The buildings outside seemed so futuristic, they glowed in all sorts of cool colors, and the metal seemed to reflect the entire spectrum. There weren't any plants that I could see, nor could I see the sky, there was no real way to tell what this place looked like outside of what had been built here.

"There you go, darling, all done. Would you like a loli?" The doctor asked, holding out a lollipop.

Not knowing what the flavors here would be like or how my body would react to the ingredients, I politely declined. The medical assistant returned and worked to get rid of the last group of spent injections while the doctor put the treat away in her pocket. She went to say something to me, but a little beeping sound coming from her pocket interrupted her. From there, she produced a little square that I could only describe as a holopad. It glowed a light blue and hovered just above her right hand as her left played with things I couldn't see. She smiled suddenly and put the item away.

"His Majesty is ready to see you now," She said, gently taking my hand between hers.

"Who?"

"Our leader! The man who made all of this possible, you're very lucky," She explained, lifting me from the chair.

I kept quiet as she led me out into a hallway, then down

another, up a flight of stairs, and around a corner until I came to a weird tube looking elevator. Standing by the door were two men holding sticks that flashed and sizzled when we approached, they stepped aside and pressed a button to open the door. The doctor gave me a reassuring smile before gently pushing me in through the door. I turned around to face the outside; the doctor waved goodbye at me and stepped back.

The two men stepped inside like your typical soldiers, methodical almost robotic, and pressed the top button on the wall. Below me, the floor lifted with a mechanical whir, nearly giving me motion sickness. It moved unlike anything on Earth, so smooth and fast. It was making me nervous. I had to shut my eyes to keep from getting sick. This was probably a bad idea since I could have taken the chance to look around, but I don't think it would have gone over well if I puked on their beautiful fancy elevator. I nearly jumped for joy when we finally stopped, and the machine dinged to let us know.

When the doors opened, I waited for the soldiers to step out, but they didn't. They gestured for me to go ahead, bowing as I stepped off. If it wasn't embarrassing enough, my foot slipped a little on the nicely polished floor, almost sending me off my feet. Luckily I recovered, hoping they didn't see.

"Woah," I whispered as I looked around the massive room I'd been brought to.

There were all sorts of fancy furniture everywhere, shining in the bright lights that came in from the massive windows that filled the farthest wall. I could see buildings below us, their lights creating a brilliant luminescence. Small little space ships came flying by the windows, heading to who knows what with a sense of urgency. Looking all the way up, I saw thousands of stars, all sorts of amazing colors and sizes, that I didn't

84

recognize. Brilliant splots of light and color painted the sky, further reminding me that I had no clue where I was.

"Beautiful, isn't it?" A voice said right next to me.

"Ah!" I screamed, bumping into a pedestal.

Both I and the pedestal went falling to the ground. Whatever had been sitting on, it went sliding across the floor in the opposite direction. Before I hit the ground, two hands grabbed my arm and pulled me up.

"Oh shit! I'm so sorry; I shouldn't have snuck up on you. I'm just so excited," The person said as they helped me get my footing.

Looking up, I found a man standing in front of me wearing more of those spacy clothes, but his looked even more expensive and luxurious. He was a great deal taller than me. My head only made it to his chest. I slowly panned upward and started to inspect his face. He had really sharp features like the action characters you see on tv. His eyes looked so dramatic and animalistic; it was hard to meet their gaze even when he was looking at me with a soft expression. His hair fell in layers to around medium length, the same color as mine.

"Just look at you, you've got your mother's eyes but definitely my hair," He said, reaching up to touch my hair.

I took a step back nervously, still unsure of what was going on.

"Ah! There I go again, and I wanted so much to make a good impression," He sighed, pulling his hands back. "My name is AL1TH1US, I'm your father," he finally said, holding out his hand for me to take.

For my entire life up until now, my "father" had just been a concept, an idea, a word. I knew I had one, biologically speaking, I had to have one, but I had no clue what he was like. Sometimes late at night, when I couldn't sleep, I would make up a father. He was tall, great at sports, hilarious, and he loved taking me to get ice cream like the other kids' dads did. He worked at a law firm, a bank; he was a pilot, a navy man, an astronaut. He bought me a dog, a fish, a cat. He volunteered at an old folks' home, an animal shelter, the hospital, and everyone said he was such a good guy. He and my mom broke up because she didn't like how much time he was spending away from home.

It was peculiar realizing that the man in front of me was the one who I'd been speculating about for all these years, like learning you had a third limb or something, a total paradigm shift. I wasn't disappointed, he was tall, handsome, and looked strong enough to give me a piggyback ride, all good qualities in a father. The place we're standing in is grander than anything I'd ever imagined for him, his clothes more beautiful than anything I could have made up.

"Sorry, I'm sure this is a lot for you to take in," My father said, breaking the silence.

"It's a little overwhelming, not going to lie."

I imagined all the years I lived without him. All the father's days where I made cards for my mother instead of him, all the family portraits I'd done of just my mother and me, imagining if he'd been there. What would life have been like with him?

"We can talk more at dinner. I'm sure you're starving," He said, placing a hand on my shoulder.

"Now that you mention it. Wait, where's Nikki?" I said, the mention of food reminding me of my freeloading friend that I hadn't seen since the incident on the ship.

"Who?"

"Nikki, she was the human on the ship with us," I explained.

"Human? You mean the Earthling?"

86

"Yes, she's my friend. I can't just leave her."

"Well, if she's your friend, then I would be more than happy for her to join us."

Turning from me, he pulled out a holopad similar to the one the doctor had. He pushed a button on it then a few more. A person's face appeared, and he began to speak.

"Bring her up to the dining hall. She is a special guest tonight."

"Yes, your Majesty."

The person disappeared, and my father put the holopad away. He turned to me with a gentle smile, placing his hand on my back between my shoulder blades so he could lead me away.

"She woke up a little while ago and just finished up her shots. She'll be meeting us for dinner," He said as he led me back toward the elevator.

"Is she alright?"

"The doctor said she's doing great. They were worried that since she's an earthling, she might have a reaction, but they said she did fantastically."

Pressing a button on the elevator, my father stood next to me, looking straight ahead with a bright smile on his face. From what I've heard about him, this is not at all what I pictured he'd be like. He seems a lot more reasonable than I would have first thought. It makes sense, though, when I think about it, he probably wouldn't get very far if he looked like some terrifying monster. Noticing me out of the corner of his eye, he turned and gave me a big grin. Blushing at being caught, I looked down.

"I've been waiting a long time for this," He said, looking out through the glass.

"For what?"

"Getting to meet you. I've been searching the galaxy trying to find you, and now you're finally here. My son, my darling….

Wait, I forgot to ask your name," He said, slapping his hand over his mouth.

He looked so ashamed for forgetting. I almost laughed.

"Galileo. That's my name," I replied.

"Gal-li-le-o," He said each part slowly, testing it out.

After giving it a thoughtful pause, he grinned.

"Earth has such a strange naming system; I love it!"

The elevator doors opened, revealing the same aliens from before. This time, they bowed deeply as we walked by, their eyes never meeting ours. He led me down a hallway with floors so polished they looked like one big mirror. After a few twists and turns, I could hear familiar laughter coming from behind an imposing silver door.

"Haha! And what's this?" Nikki asked a chef in an apron, pointing to these weird egg looking things on a serving platter.

"Boiled Squelch eggs. They taste best this time of year," He replied, setting down a plate of spiky looking vegetables.

"Oh! And those?"

"Spiky Duran. Its sweet flavor is elevated when mixed with the proper spices."

"No way!"

Nikki looked like she was having the time of her life, which is probably the case. She looked happier than I've ever seen her at dinner. When the two of us walked in, she waved at me.

"Galileo! Look at all this stuff; it's space food and not that stuff they sell in stores in the bags but real-life space food!" She said, snapping hundreds of pictures on her phone.

"We're in the middle of space, and you're getting excited over food? You never change," I teased.

"Shut up! How about you and your friend come join me?" She said, gesturing to the empty seats to her right.

"Oh, this isn't my friend; it's-" I stopped myself, not comfortable enough yet to say "my dad," but he did it for me.

"I'm Galileo's father, and you must be Nikki," He said, walking over to shake her hand politely.

She gave me a look as she shook his hand, one that said, "Holy shit! It's your dad!". With formalities exchanged, I took my place next to Nikki, and my father took the seat at the head of the table. I was in the position immediately to his right, then Nikki, leaving the chair to his left open. I wondered who it was for since it had a plate sitting in front of it, so surely someone was coming. The answer appeared before I even asked in the form of a girl who appeared to be about my age with unnaturally white hair.

She entered the room quickly, pushing the doors aside forcefully before approaching the table. Before sitting down, she bowed.

"Your majesty, your highness," She began. "My sincerest apologies for my lateness, my prior appointment took longer than I expected."

"Don't worry, R0S4L1N4; we just got here as well. Take a seat and come meet my son," My dad said, gesturing to the seat to his left.

There were a lot more seats at the table, but none of them had plates in front of them. I guess it's only going to be the four of us. I went to mention it but was cut off by my father.

"Galileo, I'd like you to meet your adopted sister, R0S4L1N4. I adopted her after her father's death, she's not much older than you," He said, gesturing between the two of us.

As she stood to shake my hand, the chefs walked around and started serving the food, finishing the process by grating things on top or mixing stuff in.

"A pleasure. I look forward to getting to know you, Galileo," She said with a practiced roboticism, lacking in emotion.

"And next to him is his friend Nikki, she's an Earthling," My father added, picking up his utensil to start eating.

"A pleasure, any friend of Galileo's, is a friend of mine."

"Same to you. Shall we?" Nikki replied, gesturing to the food.

R0S4L1N4, whom I'm going to call Rosalina, nodded, and sat down, taking her utensil in her hand. Nikki watched her use it, cleverly hiding her lack of knowledge. Once she seemed to grasp it, she went about trying the many things on her plate. No matter how strange it all looked, she slurped it up happily.

"So are mom and the rest of them coming?" I asked.

At the mention, Rosalina's eyebrow twitched ever so slightly. It was almost impossible to notice unless you were hyper-focused like I was.

"I'm afraid not. They haven't finished with all the prep work they've been doing, to make sure they have an easy time reentering society," He replied, taking another bite.

"Oh, well, when they're done, can I see them?"

"Of course, you'll be the first to know."

His response didn't reassure me, but I didn't want to press. Who knows? I haven't gotten a read on his personality, so there's no telling how he might react to my questioning. Turning to the plate in front of me, I swallowed nervously. The utensil to my left looked kind of like a fork, but with wider tongs. I picked it up and went to stab a piece of a harmless-looking vegetable. My teeth sank into it easily; the juices coating my tongue as I chewed through the delicate plant matter. The taste was kind of like a zucchini, but if you mixed it with a green bean. Whatever flavoring they'd put on it was a little spicy, nothing overwhelming though, I could still enjoy the taste without feeling like my tongue was on fire.

Next, I went after what looked like a slice of meat, the juices pooling in little crevices on its surface.

"So, Galileo, tell me about yourself," My father interrupted the silence.

"Like what?"

"Whatever you want to tell me, we've got three solar years to catch up on, might as well get started," He laughed.

"Where to start? Um, I like techno music," I began.

"What does that sound like?"

"Well, it's all made by machines, so like, non-traditional. Let me see," I said, pulling out my phone.

To save space, I don't usually download songs I stream them, but I do have a few of my favorites saved from the one time I tried using one of those youtube to MP3 converters. My computer crashed a bunch of times, but I got my songs, and that's what matters. Clicking my absolute favorite, I set my phone on the table; the techno sounds soon following. Rosalina and my father both looked down and paused their eating to listen. Next to me, Nikki started to wiggle along with the music; this was also one of her favorites. She was the one who introduced me to this artist. I still remember the day we were sitting on the floor in my room, and she pulled her phone out to show me. The rest of the afternoon, we spent bobbing our heads to whatever she put on next.

My dad gave my phone a perplexed look, but he didn't seem angry. He waved his head back and forth, testing how it felt to try and move to the beat.

"That certainly is different from anything we have here, but I like it! Maybe I could take you to a concert soon," He said, his face lighting up.

"There's the Solar Wind festival in a few months, that one should be good," Rosalina added, already making the arrangements on her holopad.

"Lovely, that should be a blast."

"Now it's my turn," I said.

"For what?"

"Asking questions, I want to learn more about you, too," I explained.

Dad grinned widely, placing his chin on his hands.

"Go ahead. I'm happy to answer anything you want to know."

Several more pointed questions came to mind first. Why does mom hate you? Are you an evil dictator? Are you going to kill mom and her friends? Have I been injected with some crazy like you serum that will make me the perfect little son? But I chose to keep all of those inside of me, wanting to play it cool.

"So, what do you do?" I asked, taking a sip of my drink, which tasted like strawberries.

"I run this place. I'm the king, for lack of a better word. You'll learn more about this place soon, I've got a lot to catch you up on it seems," He laughed.

"Yeah, mom never told me about where she was from."

"She tried to say she was from Earth to keep this all a secret from Galileo," Nikki added.

"Not on purpose though, I don't think."

"I can understand why. Your mother wasn't a fan of The Senate. I bet you already knew that," My father said.

"I don't know why. This place seems cool!" Nikki cheered, taking a big bite.

"Thank you, Earthling. I can't wait to learn about where you two came from, from what I've heard it sounds… rustic."

The last word, he puzzled over for a long time, trying to find a way to say, "Your home sounds like it's full of lower lifeforms wandering around with primitive technology" in a way that didn't insult us. I caught the tone in his voice, but it seemed Nikki did not.

"Oh, for sure, compared to this place. You guys have things people on Earth have only dreamed about."

"How tragic, perhaps in the future we could go visit your home, bring them new technologies."

"That sounds ama-"

"Maybe one day," I interrupted. "But not anytime soon, we've got too much catching up to do."

I made up an excuse on the spot, it wasn't overly convincing, but it seemed to buy me some time. Mom had a reason for not liking this place. Bringing them to Earth could spell disaster, and I couldn't let all the innocent people back home suffer.

"You're right, son. Tomorrow is going to be nothing but father-son bonding time. I've got so much to show you!"

"I can't wait. Better get a good night's sleep then," I said, my plate now empty.

Some of the people from before came to clean up the plates, swiftly taking them from in front of us and wiping away any mess we might have made. When I stood up, my father walked up behind me, placing a hand on my shoulder.

"Here, let me take you to your room, R0S4, would you take the Earthling to hers?"

She nodded, holding her arm out for Nikki to go ahead. Nikki smiled, heading that way before stopping and turning back to me.

"Sleep, good space cadet!" She said, waving goodbye to me.

"You too, Milky Way, hold on that was dumb," I laughed, rubbing the back of my neck.

"Idiot," She laughed, turning to follow Rosalina.

When I turned back around, I nearly ran into my father, who was looking between Nikki and myself with a tiny smile on his face. He shook it off, leading me back toward the elevator. We went down several hallways before coming to a stop at a metal sliding door in the middle of a hall full of pictures I couldn't see from where we stood.

My father pushed a button on the wall on a panel I hadn't seen before, causing the two doors to slide apart with a gentle swish. The room behind the door was big, like the kind of place you'd stay in at a nice hotel. On one wall was a wide bed, big enough for at least three people with a red blanket emblazoned with a symbol I didn't recognize. On the wall, farthest from me, was a massive panel of windows, finally allowing me to get a good look at this strange planet. The buildings were so far below. I could just barely see their roofs, the metal reflecting the light from the millions of stars in the dark sky.

Other than the bed, there wasn't much furniture. There were two doors which I assumed led to a bathroom and a closet, but I would have to check. The lights above came from brilliant little orbs; I wasn't sure if they were made of glass or if they even had a physical shape.

"Sorry it's so boring, I wanted to make sure you had total control of what your room looked like," My father said.

"No, no, it's great. I can already see it. This place'll be perfect in no time," I replied, gesturing around to emphasize my plans.

"I'm sure it will be. I'll leave you to get comfortable now. We've got a lot to do tomorrow, so be sure to get plenty of rest."

Sitting down on the bed, I nodded to him. He walked up to where I was and held out his arms for a hug.

"May I?" He asked.

"S-Sure," I replied.

It was weird having my dad ask to hug me, heck it was strange just having a dad, but when he wrapped his arms around me, I was filled with this weird feeling of contentedness. Suddenly, it was as if a hole inside of me that I didn't even know existed was filled. The hug felt so natural, and yet utterly new at the same time. When we pulled away from each other, I didn't know what to say.

"Sleep well, I love you," He said as he stepped outside, pausing in the door frame for a moment.

"Love you too," I replied, prompting him to grin and close the door, which slid shut with the same hiss.

Even though I spent most of the day unconscious, I was exhausted. With all that happened today, I was completely drained. It was probably more of a mental tiredness, but still, it had me slumped.

There was a change of clothes waiting in the closet. They were the spacy type, and a size or two too big, but they would do. I'll have to be fitted for clothes anyway, that'll probably come tomorrow.

After a quick trip to the bathroom, I was changed and ready to sleep. The bed was impossibly soft, better than those mattresses at the mall that the salesperson has to use a remote to activate. As I curled up under the blankets, I looked up at the moon visible from my window. It was blueish, and much larger than the moon back home. I wondered if mom was looking at the same thing right this moment. Hopefully, I'll get to see her tomorrow. Then we can sort all of this nonsense out.

Once the door had shut, and his son was no longer in view, AL1TH1US's entire demeanor changed. The sweet fatherly kindness he'd shown his son was gone, replaced with a scowl and an air of menace that filled the whole hall. Anyone who passed him kept their head down, afraid of becoming a victim of his rage. He walked down several halls, rode down several floors, before finally coming to a stop at the dungeon.

Matilda's friends were being housed in a different part of the jail from her; he knew better than to keep them anywhere near each other. He passed their cells on the way, their bodies suspended in a liquid that kept them unconscious but functioning.

In the most secure cell of the royal dungeon, Matilda was strapped down to a table surrounded by guns all pointed at her. If she moved too much, an electric shock would shoot through the straps, she discovered that one herself. When AL1TH1US entered the room, the guns moved aside to let him through.

The two looked at each other with intense glares. Should anything cross between them, the sharpness of their gazes would surely slice it. Only the sound of his footsteps echoed throughout the massive cell.

"I can't believe you. Do you have any idea how dangerous that was?! You could have been killed. Our son could have died! The horrors you must have put him through out there on some primitive planet full of savages, what do you have to say for yourself?!" He yelled, getting right in her face.

A moment of silence passed as he waited for her answer. She pursed her lips and spat with as much force as she could manage, spraying a mouthful of spit onto him. AL1TH1US stepped back, wiping his face as he groaned in disgust.

"Ha! Been saving that for hours," Matilda yelled in triumph.

With the spit gone, AL1TH1US glared at her before raising his hand and slapping her hard across the face. The force knocked her head to the side and left a red mark in the shape of his hand. There would no doubt be an ugly bruise there the next day.

"You think this is funny, don't you? This isn't some game you ignorant bi-," He stopped himself, taking a deep breath.

"The stakes are much higher, M4. You have our son to think about now and his little friend. It'd be a shame if something were to happen to them because of your ill manner," He threatened.

"My name is Matilda, and I dare you to lay a finger on either of those kids. I'd shove my foot so far down your throat-"

"You're in no position to be making threats, *Matilda*," he pronounced her name as if it were a slur. "If I were you, I'd be a good little girl and do as I say."

"Or what?" She growled.

"Or we'll just have to have a repeat of our little trip back from the Omega Quasar, although this time, you won't be escaping."

His words rendered her silent, the memory of what happened shook her to the core. She looked away, thinking hard about what to do next.

"Now tomorrow you're going to lie for me, you're going to pretend that everything is wonderful in front of our son, alright? Otherwise, I'll lock you back up and never let you see him again."

With that, he turned and left the room, leaving her to think about what he said. He was right; there was so much more at stake this time, innocent children she had to think about. It didn't matter what happened to her, but she wasn't going to let anything happen to her son or his friend. For now, she was just going to have to go along with it, waiting for her opportunity.

9

Chapter 9

I awoke to the sound of an electronic chime, two notes, one low then one high. Sitting up, I rubbed my eyes and looked around. At first, I didn't know where I was, but then the memories from yesterday came rushing back, reminding me.

The closet door opened on its own, and a pair of shiny space clothes slid out for me to take. The material felt amazing, so light like I was holding nothing. I couldn't put a name to the color, it was grayish, with a shimmery rainbow effect going on with pieces that seemed to reflect the entire spectrum at once. When I put it on, it fit perfectly even though it had looked a bit small originally.

Another chime sounded when I pushed the closet door shut, this time coming from the bathroom. Waiting for me was a toothbrush with toothpaste already on it. I picked it up, examining the bristles and paste. It appeared brand new, the hairs were still perfectly straight, each one in its place, the toothpaste was blue with small darker blue bits dotting the edge. It tasted like blueberry, which surprised me. I was not expecting to taste blueberry this far out in space. The darker bits were grainy, scraping the plaque off my teeth just like back home.

As I brushed, a weird piece of machinery came down, brushing my hair for me. Once I finished, a cup appeared from inside the mirror, already full of water. I gargled and spat, returning the cup to its place.

The water here tasted odd. It wasn't bad, it was just weird. It wasn't just pure water taste, there was something else there, something different from what I was used to.

Another chime sounded, and the door to my room slid open. Rosalina was standing there next to my father. She stepped in first, making room for my father. Behind them were several security guards who stood at attention with their spears in hand, waiting for a chance to use them.

"Good morning Galileo," My father said, holding out his arms for me.

"Good morning," I replied.

"Did you sleep well?"

"Oh yes, the bed was really comfortable, it's a lot better than my bed at home," I laughed.

"I'm glad we've got a big day ahead of us."

"Is Nikki coming?" I asked.

"Absolutely, we're going to pick her up right now," My father replied, placing his hand on my shoulder and leading me out.

We went down a few hallways and came to a stop outside of a door that was smaller than mine. From inside, I could hear Nikki's delighted screams. I rolled my eyes and adjusted in place. Dad placed his hand on the panel, and the door slid open. When Nikki noticed it was me, she came running over.

"Dude, look! I'm wearing space clothes!" She yelled, pointing to her outfit.

MY MOM THE INTERGALACTIC TERRORIST

Her's was similar to mine, but it was a light pink instead, not nearly as shiny. The machine had done her hair in her usual poofs, which were perfectly symmetrical. I doubt they would have been that perfect if she'd done them by herself.

"I don't know why you're so excited about a pair of shiny pajamas," I teased.

"How dare you? This is fancy alien clothes, not pajamas, you cretin!" She scolded, hitting me on the shoulder.

"How do you know they're fancy? For all, you know these might be considered peasant clothes around here," I questioned.

I had her there. She lifted her hand up and opened her mouth to reply, but quickly shut it, looking to the side as she tried to come up with a rebuttal. Lacking one, she quickly crossed her arms and changed the subject.

"Did you get a good look at these rooms? Aren't they amazing?"

"Yeah, they sure are ages ahead of us in terms of technology. It's like something out of a movie you'd make me watch."

"Goodness, your planet lacked even the basic necessities?" Rosalina interrupted.

I hadn't noticed her approach. She creeps so unsuspectingly, like the employees at a department store that you don't see until they suddenly say, "Is there anything I can help you with?" scaring you. That probably comes in handy when you're an assistant like she is.

"R0S4! Be polite," My father warned.

"Oh no, it's okay. We have running water and electricity, but we don't have robots that help us get ready. We have to do that by ourselves," I explained.

"How archaic," Rosa added, earning her a nudge on the side.

"Being able to take care of yourself is an excellent skill to have.

Just imagine if you were lost out on some distant planet, you'd have no idea how to keep yourself clean." My dad said.

That got me thinking. Now that I see what mom came from, I can kind of tell why she always struggled with stuff on Earth. For me, it was easy because Earth was all I'd ever known, but she had to relearn how to do everything. I want to know what that was like for her, and why she did that. What was so bad about this place that she subjected herself to all of that to "protect" me?

A holoscreen appeared right next to my father's shoulder, accompanied by a loud ringing. He turned, checked to see who it was, then pulled the holopad towards him, holding it up to his ear like a cellphone.

"Yes? Oh... she can't. What a shame. Will she at least be joining us for dinner? Alright, thank you," He said, ending the call and dismissing the pad.

From the look on his face, I could tell the call was bad news. Looking up at me, he gave me a sad but carrying look.

"Sorry, Galileo, your mother has some business to attend to, so I'm afraid she won't be joining us today until dinner."

"Alright, can't wait to see her again."

"Of course, let's get started with our plans for the day. There's so much I want to show you," My father said, his excitement evident in the way his shoulders tensed.

He went to lead the way, Nikki pushing past me and staying right next to his side like a loyal puppy. I hesitated a moment, still worried about my mother. It was hard to shake the feeling of nervousness that filled my stomach, it was weird doing anything, knowing that I had no idea how she was or if she was okay.

Rosa noticed, giving me a sideways glance.

"Come along, your highness." She said, waving her hand forward.

"Ah, sorry," I said, taking a few steps.

She stayed behind, closer to where I was. While Nikki talked my father's ear off, I watched, observing how my father behaved, how he laughed at whatever she said, and listened with interest. It was just like all the other fathers I'd seen before; being kind to their children's friends even though they were talking nonsense.

"Don't let your mother's opinion of him stop you from making your own," Rosa said, breaking my concentration.

"Sorry, what?" I said, even though I'd heard her just fine.

"I know your mother has probably told you plenty of terrible things about him, surely nothing but lies, but don't let that get in the way of you making your own opinion," She explained.

"You're right, she did say some things, but don't worry, I'll give him a chance," I replied, hoping to appease her.

She gave me another sideways glance before looking down at her holopad, acting like I was unimportant. After pressing a few buttons, she spoke.

"Your mother lies, always search for your own truth."

I gulped, looking away nervously. She's so serious, no matter what I say, she makes me look so uneducated and silly. With a nod, I hurried ahead, catching up to Nikki and my father.

When I got there, Nikki was asking him about their names.

"What does it all mean?"

"Well, our names tell us things about each other. The first letter tells us what planet that person was born on and based on that the following series of letters and numbers tell us things like when they were born, who their parents were, and all sorts of other things."

"What planet were you born on?"

"I, like every other heir, was born on Arrowyn. It's tradition."

"Is it bad that I wasn't?" I asked nervously.

He turned and looked at me thoughtfully, giving me a tender smile.

'No, no, it's an old tradition. Maybe some of the traditionalists will be annoyed, but it doesn't really matter. You're my son, the first of our family to be born outside of our known universe."

That made me feel at least a little better. At least he doesn't see me as a disappointment. Even if he does turn out to be evil, I still don't want to be a disappointment to my father.

After a quick stop for breakfast, we headed back down several halls. There were so many twists, and turns it made my head spin. I had no clue how anyone could even dream about remembering so many directions, but it seemed to my dad to be no big deal.

In front of our path, I could see a door unlike any I'd seen up until that point. All the others were sleek, with no identifying features, like the doors on an elevator, but this one had ornate designs engraved all over. It looked much older than anything else I'd seen in this place as if, maybe it was somewhere else and had been brought here.

This one slid open much slower when my dad put his hand up to the wall panel. Stepping inside, he gestured for us to go inside. The three of us went in before him, the guards staying behind, and my father joining us right before the door closed.

Inside was a massive room, so long I couldn't see the end and so tall the roof looked hazy. On every side as far as the eye could see were massive paintings, life-sized renditions of several people. Below each was a holopad with their name, birth, and death date, and different tabs you could click to learn more.

I spun around, taking in as much as I could. It was overwhelming but so amazing, it took my breath away.

"This is the hall of kings. In this hall, is a painting of every heir to the throne as far back as we can trace. These are your ancestors," My father explained, gesturing to the entire room.

"Wow," I gasped.

I walked up to the closest painting, that of a man wearing a costly looking suit and cape. On top of his head of dark hair sat a crown; in his right hand, he held a sword, the sheath resting on his left hip. The pad below said "AD4M".

"This is our distant grandfather, AD4M. He was the one who discovered this planet and named it Malacia after the native woman he took as his bride. Next to him is his daughter ALT14, she funded the research that helped us perfect space travel," My father began.

He put a hand on my shoulder and led me down the hall.

"Here, let's get to some more recent portraits."

The passage of time was evident. As we walked, the traditional paint portraits were replaced with digital ones, huge pictures that were staged just like the paintings. They all had the same serious look on their faces, looking down at me with little interest. Their eyes were facing the future, full of wisdom and thought. They all made me feel small.

At the end of the portrait line was my father's to the right and a man I'd never seen before's on the left. According to the pad below, his name was "AR7W1N".

"This is my father, your grandfather. He died when I was young, killed by terrorists. Here, the newer ones are much more advanced," He said, reaching up.

When he touched the portrait, it reacted. He swiped his finger to the left, pulling a new picture up onto the screen.

This one wasn't staged like the portrait, it was candid, showing my grandfather standing next to a woman, a younger version of dad in the middle.

"Here, I am with my parents. This is probably the last photo we took together, my mother wasn't around much, focusing more on exploration than family. She died when her ship landed on hostile territory."

There was pain evident in my father's eyes when he talked about his mother. It was apparent that he was still hurt about what happened, but he quickly shrugged it off, moving over to his portrait.

"Enough about my side of the family. Look! This photo was taken the day of my coronation, you can see your maternal grandfather over to the right. He served as General under both my father and me."

"Where's mom?" I asked.

"She was too young to be there, probably back home with her nursery robot."

"What about my grandmother?"

"She died while she was pregnant with your mom."

"How did Matilda survive?" Nikki asked, interrupting.

"The doctors removed her, placing her in an incubator where she continued to grow and develop until she was able to survive on her own."

"That's amazing! We didn't have anything like that on Earth. Heck, we couldn't even dream of doing something like that," Nikki replied.

"Really? How sad."

"What did the incubator look like?" I asked.

"Would you like to see one?"

"Sure!" Nikki and I replied enthusiastically.

105

"Then follow me," My dad laughed.

He led the way, and Nikki and I stayed close behind. As usual, Rosa kept her distance, constantly typing on that holopad. I wanted to know what she was up to, but when I looked at the pad, it all looked like nonsense to me.

The guards outside perked up when we opened the door, following us once again, this time up a few floors and down a few halls. Every window we passed, I looked out , trying to see more of this planet. It was bright out to where I could finally see the buildings clearly, and they looked pretty much like skyscrapers. There were even more spaceships flying in between buildings this time; they looked like fruit flies, they were so plentiful.

We didn't have to go very far this time. The door was once again sleek and streamlined, just like all the others. When my father opened the door, a strong, chemical cleaner smell hit me.

Inside were several little pod looking things filled with a bluish liquid. Some had babies suspended in them with wires and tubes connected to their bodies. For the most part, the babies were humanoid, although some were so early in development that it was hard to tell, others were some other strange alien species. Occasionally, they would move, kicking their tiny legs or wiggling their arms in their sleep.

Nikki ran over to one of the pods containing one of the weirdest looking alien babies, of course, and pressed her face against it. She had a massive grin on her face.

"This is amazing! Just wait until the president sees this. I bet we'll have three, no four of these facilities set up in every hospital around the country by the time...." Nikki began to rant as she took countless pictures of the developing babies.

She was kind enough to turn the flash off at least. While she did that, my father bent down and whispered in my ear.

"This is where I met your mother, although she doesn't remember."

"Really."

"Mhm, It was over there. That pod is new, but it's in the same place as hers was." He said, pointing to a pod close to the center of the room.

"You see, only the upper class have their children incubated here, because of its close proximity to the capital, this facility is reserved to ensure that the elites don't have to travel far to see their developing children. Being the daughter of The Senate's general, your mother was brought here to be incubated. Her father stayed here for days, never sleeping or eating, watching your mother. I guess after the loss of his wife, he was scared he'd lose her too. Anyway, my father brought me here to visit him, and while they talked, I watched your mother."

"Was mom an ugly baby?" I joked.

"No," He laughed. "Well, not by baby standards. I remember her kicking a lot, she was a very athletic baby."

I laughed at the thought of mom swimming around in the goo. Is that something they do in the womb, or does that only happen in these artificial ones? How does this affect babies? Does spending the entire gestation period inside the mother have any benefits over this alternative? My mind was spinning with questions, but I couldn't decide on what to ask. Thankfully Nikki came over and broke the silence.

"What other cool medical things do you guys have? Are there other rooms we can check out?"

"We'll have to save that for another day, we've got a few more errands to run." He replied, leading us out the door.

The next place we went to was a massive room filled with

ships. There was a big door for the spacecrafts to go in and out of, and occasionally one would. Unlike the planes back home, these didn't blow off as much air, so they didn't jostle our hair around.

Aliens of all shapes, sizes, and colors moved all around us, hopping out of ships, repairing, or heading to their next assignment. Seeing my father, some paused to salute while others gave him a hasty bow, their awaiting business too important to delay. The sound of Nikki's phone camera was just barely audible over all the chatter.

"Right this way, there's something I want to give you," My father said, leading us toward the wall of the hanger.

There, just a few meters from the door was a massive, sleek-looking spaceship. In shape, it was cylindrical with very subtle curves and bends. I couldn't see any gaps where pieces of metal touched like it was all one continuous piece. Just like mom's ship, it was impossibly shiny, reflecting small rainbows across its surface.

"It is customary for a father to give his child their first ship once they turn a certain age. Your grandfather gave your mother Starhopper, now it's my turn to give you this. I had the finest engineers work to build you this around the time you'd be turning 2 solar years, even though I didn't know if I'd ever find you," He explained, I could see the glint of tears in his eyes.

"What's it called?" I asked.

"I didn't name it, that honor goes to you."

"So cool, hold on, I should vlog this," Nikki interjected, pulling out her phone.

"Hey everybody, it's ya girl, here in space with my best friend who we now know is an Alien. His father just gave him a super cool spaceship, and he's about to name it. How do you feel,

Galileo?" She asked, pointing the phone at me.

Unsure what to say, I waved, then tried to think of what to name the ship. Mom has Starhopper, which I think is pretty cool, but I don't want to copy that. I could reference something like a tv show, but that's lame. It needs to be cool and badass, something I could be proud of. Finally, it hit me.

"The Assayer, how about that?"

"For those of you who don't know, The Assayer was a book written by the astronomer Galileo, he's made an awful pun," Nikki spoke into her phone.

"Oh, hush, I like it."

"Of course you do, you have a bad sense of humor."

"I think it's great, son," My father said, giving me a thumbs up.

"Thanks, dad."

My dad placed his hand on the side of the ship, just like mom did, causing a panel to appear. Next to the panel, a door appeared and opened, releasing the pressure with a sharp hiss. A ramp shot out and landed in front of us, providing us with a way in.

"After you," Dad said.

I went first with Nikki right behind me. Her phone was still recording, so she pointed it left and right as we walked in while narrating the entire thing.

"We are now entering the space ship."

"Nikki, they have eyes." I laughed.

Inside, the ship was dark. We looked for the light switch to no avail. It wasn't until dad hit a button on another panel that we realized there were no switches. All the lights came on, revealing a large control room similar to the one in mom's ship but with fewer chairs and a much more minimalist design.

There was a similar massive panel of buttons, but these had different marks on them and were in different places.

Even though the ship was supposed to have been old, it was immaculately clean inside. There wasn't a single sign of dust anywhere, no dirt, not even a streak from any form of cleaner. It was unnaturally perfect.

"Do you like it?" My father asked.

"Of course, it's amazing. I've never seen anything like this before in my life."

"Wonderful! I had our top minds working on it. This ship has every safety feature imaginable, all the latest technology, and a power source twice the size of the average ship. It is the finest The Senate has to offer."

"Yes, the ship your mother was given has a power source only a quarter of the size of this ship, and at the time it was built, it was the top of the line. Not only that, this ship is powered by a neutron star where your mother's was powered by a red dwarf," Rosalina added.

Based on what little I remember from astronomy, that sounded really good. I've seen how amazing Starhopper is and if this thing is that much better, then it must really be something to behold.

"Would you like to try it out?" My dad asked, gesturing to the control panel.

"Me, fly a spaceship? I haven't even driven a car before I could never-" I began.

Across from me, Nikki gave a thumbs up from behind her phone with a cheesy smile on her face. If I remember correctly, she once told me that one day she'd like to fly a spaceship. It was on her bucket list, and it didn't matter if it was a flying saucer or one of NASA's as long as it could get her into space.

I would never let her fly this, though, because I have seen her try to drive before. She ran into her garage and her mailbox before she even got it out of the driveway. There is no way she could get this thing off the ground without hurting at least one person.

"I'll try," I sighed.

The look of glee on my father's face was adorable as he ran over to stand beside me. Rosalina and Nikki went to take a seat in one of the chairs behind us. I heard two distinct seatbelt clicks, letting me know they had no faith in me.

"Alright, son, place your hand on the part of the screen that has the long line of bars of decreasing size, that's the throttle. Good, now slowly move your hand upward along the bars, this will engage the thrusters slowly, allowing for a slow and steady ascension."

I tried to follow his orders, moving from the bottom bar to the second with what I thought was enough hesitation, but judging by the way the ship lurched upward, wasn't enough. Panicking, I overcorrected, jumping back down to the first bar, which caused the craft to fall suddenly, giving me that stomach in chest feeling you get when you're on a rollercoaster with a steep drop.

My father just laughed and placed his hand on my shoulder. I was expecting him to yell at me or grab the controls, but he just laughed, gently rubbing my shoulder in support.

"It's okay, just relax. Nobody is perfect their first time flying."

With a deep breath, I tried again, moving even slower this time. It was still a harsh transition, but not as bad as before, which was progress. Nikki cheered me on from behind, clapping and whooping while still holding the phone in place.

Their support made me feel confident, combined with how

well the ship was holding its place, I felt like I could try moving it forward. I pushed the button that indicated forward, which I quickly realized was a big mistake. The entire vessel shot forward, nearly knocking me off my feet. My stomach hit the panel, making my hand slip, which in turn caused the ship to lower suddenly.

Lucky for me, my father was quick and caught me before I fell flat.

"That was a great first try son, we'll get more into flying another day, wouldn't want to hurt ourselves," He teased as he helped me up.

"Yeah, I'll just put her back down," I replied.

I moved my hand super slow once again, but I knew I'd done something wrong when I heard the horrible metallic screech it made as it touched the ground. Nikki and I made shocked and frightened expressions, but dad and Rosalina smiled.

"Little rough on the landing there kiddo, but it's alright. New flyers are always rough on their landing gear, you just have to replace them often to make up for that," Dad reassured me.

"Nice flying, space cadet. A real natural," Nikki laughed, getting out of her seat and running over to punch me on the shoulder.

"Says the girl who hit a house."

"Hey, I didn't see it."

"It was sitting still!"

The two of us laughed, leaning against each other for support. Lifting up the phone, Nikki got us both in the shot.

"And this has been, our first attempt at flying a spaceship. Nikki and Galileo signing off," She said, ending the video and turning off her phone.

"Wonderful, now that we've done that, I bet you two are

hungry."

"I could eat."

"Great, dinner will probably be ready by the time we get there," My father said, leading us off the ship.

We walked all the way back to the dining room from before, laughing and chatting. It was much more relaxed this time. I guess that flying experience had really loosened up some of the tension between us all. Nikki and Rosalina talked and looked at things on her holopad while I talked about flying with my dad. He told me all sorts of funny stories about when he was learning to fly.

We could smell the food before we got there. It filled the hallway several corridors down, and it was heavenly. I hadn't realized how hungry I was, that little bit we had for breakfast wasn't doing it for me anymore.

A guard opened the door for us, letting us see inside. I noticed my mother right away, sitting in the chair to the right of the table's head. When she turned to look at us, I saw the bruise on the side of her face.

"Mom!" I shouted excitedly, hoping not to make a big deal about the mark.

I ran over and gave her a big hug in her chair, which she happily returned. Everyone else took their seats. With the added person, our arrangement from yesterday was thrown off, but we figured it out.

Mom sat to dad's immediate right, I sat next to her, Rosalina sat to dad's left, and Nikki sat next to her, while dad remained at the head of the table. As the chefs brought out the food, I started talking to mom.

"I can't wait to tell you all about what we did today. It's been amazing."

"That's wonderful dear, sorry I missed it, I've just been so busy."

"That's okay. Hey, I don't mean to be rude or anything but, what happened to your face?"

"Oh, this?" She asked, pointing to the mark. "When they pulled me up with the tractor beam, they accidentally cut it off too soon and dropped me. I landed on my face."

She said that all with a smile and a laugh like it was nothing, but I wasn't convinced. There was no way she'd just shrug something like that off so quickly, but I didn't want to press any further and cause any drama.

"Woops, that sucks. Other than that, how have you been?" I asked as a chef set down the final dish.

"I've been alright. Had a lot to work on," She replied, scooping food onto her plate.

We all did the same, grabbing whatever looked good and pilling our plates high. It was then that I noticed her outfit. It was different from what she wore back on her ship. This outfit was skin-tight like the rest, but it had a cape on the back that connected to big shoulder pads. On her chest were several medals and patches as well as a name badge. If I had to guess, I'd say it was her old general uniform.

"Galileo tried flying a ship today for the first time, M4," My father said between bites.

"Did he? That's great."

"I wouldn't call that flying," Nikki laughed, elbowing me under the table.

"He did just fine," My father argued, standing up for me.

"I'm sure he did, he's very talented."

"You're right, our boy sure is special."

Hearing them talk like a typical set of parents threw up all sorts of red flags for me. Not three days ago, mom was talking about how much she hated him, crying in front of everyone when she told them he was my father. She would never sit here and act like this around him unless something happened.

At the end of dinner, we all stood up and pushed in our chairs. Rosa went off toward her room, and the rest stayed to say goodnight.

"I'm glad I got to spend time with you today, son."

"Me too."

"Now, if you don't mind, your mother and I are going to retire for the evening. Goodnight," He said, giving me a hug.

"Goodnight, baby," My mom followed suit.

"Goodnight, I love you guys."

"Love you too," They said in unison before turning and heading toward their rooms.

Once they were out of earshot, I grabbed Nikki's hand and turned to her.

"Come with me," I said.

I led her back to my room, making sure she paid attention to how we got there so she could get back to hers later. With us both inside, I quickly pressed the panel to shut the door. Finally, alone, I turned to her.

"Something's up."

"Clearly."

"Alright, late-night status report. Let's go through what we noticed today," I said, starting our little meeting.

Nikki sat down on the bed before listing what she noticed.

"Your dad focused a lot today on the good things about this place, showing you how much better it is here than on Earth."

"Correct, and he gave me a present. Could he be trying to distract me?"

"It's possible, but he could also just be really excited to finally have you here."

"True, but then there's the matter of mom's behavior at dinner."

"I didn't notice anything."

"Well, that's because you don't know her as I do. She was much more fidgety than usual, not to mention that mark on her face."

"Yeah, she said it happened when she fell on the floor, but I swear it looked just like a hand."

"Exactly, I thought the same thing, but I didn't want to bring too much attention to the situation."

"Right, we've got to be stealthy," Nikki replied, making weird motions with her hands like she was trying to be a ninja.

"I'm so confused!" I groaned, flopping down onto the bed.

I moaned loudly into the fabric, which muffled the sound, so it sounded more like whale noises than moaning. Nikki leaned back and laid next to me, resting her head on her hand.

"Well, man, you just keep me informed, and I'll follow you. You know I've got your back."

"Thanks, I know you've always wanted to go into space, but I doubt you wanted to get caught up in all this family drama."

"Don't worry about it. That's what friends are for. It's no different than that time you went with us on that trip to SeaWorld, and my parents got into a fight over the directions."

I didn't reply, giving her a doubtful look.

"Okay, it's a little different, but still, I'm your friend, and that's what friends do."

"Thanks, man, I owe you big for this one."

"Well, as long as you don't repay me with a joy ride in your new space ship, I think we'll be fine," She joked, getting up and heading to the door.

"Hey, at least I won't hit any houses!" I called as she exited my room.

"Irrelevant!" I heard her say as the door slid shut.

Now that she was gone, I relaxed in my bed, stretching out completely and looking up at the ceiling. Tomorrow I'd have to come up with something to figure out what was going on. This is all so overwhelming, and I can't tell who's telling the truth anymore. For now, though, all I could do is sleep.

10

Chapter 10

The next morning, the same chime woke me up. Just like before, a fresh pair of clothes appeared for me, a robot helped me brush my teeth, and my hair was brushed for me. Barely a moment after all that was done, my father appeared at the door.

"Good morning Galileo."

"Good morning, Dad."

"Are you ready to go?"

"Yeah, what's the plan for today?" I asked, stepping out of my room.

The door slid shut behind me, I turned at the sound and noticed Rosalina standing behind us. I should have figured she'd be coming with us.

"I've got special plans for us today! I'm going to teach you a bit more about my job and what I do. You're going to see everything that goes into being the leader of The Senate."

"Is Nikki coming today?"

"Not today, R0S4 suggested we let her explore our science lab. I'm sure she'd like that more than what we're doing today,"

My dad explained.

"Ok, and what about mom?"

"She's going to get some repairs done on Starhopper. Engine's blown, she'll have to replace that; besides, she needed to update the hardware."

No matter how much I wanted to believe him, I couldn't bring myself to. Mom hated this place, I doubt she'd suddenly stop caring and drop her beliefs like that. Unless maybe she was trying to protect me.

"Alright, that's a shame. Let her know I miss her," I said, playing off my suspicion.

"I will, and she misses you too. She told me last night how she hates that she hasn't been with you during all of this. Maybe in a few days when she's done with all of her business, the three of us will do something as a family."

"Nikki too?"

'If you'd like."

"Good morning, your highness, I'm afraid I've been asked to escort your Earthling friend to the lab, so I will not be joining you today. I wish you luck," Rosalina said, bowing and walking off toward Nikki's room with two guards following behind.

I tried to say goodbye, but she was so quick to walk off; she wouldn't have heard me. To be honest, though, she probably wouldn't have noticed even if I did say something. Whatever, she needed to be with Nikki anyway. If they let her loose in an alien science lab, she'd end up hurting herself or worse, making something new to annoy me with.

Dad waved goodbye to her then led me off to wherever we were headed. We went somewhere different from where we went the day before, but I did recognize a few of the halls we passed. There were a few landmarks that I'd managed to memorize, but without them, I had no grasp on the directions in this place.

Our first stop was a big fancy looking room with loads of monitors, all covered in text that was moving so fast I couldn't follow. If I tried to focus on any one thing for too long, I ended up feeling motion sick.

"Here is one of the main information hubs for The Senate. On these computers is every bit of information in our possession. Thousands of battle plans, birth records, death records, census reports, anything you can think of passes through this room at least once," My father explained.

"That's amazing! You're able to get information from all over the Universe? How long does it take?"

"At most a few seconds."

"Really?"

"Yes. If I were to request that every planet under The Senate's control send a report of their current natural resource usage per person, I'd have them in about thirty seconds."

"I can't believe it, what else can these do?"

"Well, we can use them to search through our current database for anything in particular. For example, if I wanted to see every single person in The Senate who has three eyes, I could. If I wanted to perform a background check on someone, I could tell you every single thing that's happened to them since birth."

"That's kind of creepy," I laughed.

"It's mostly things related to their career or if they've done anything to attract our attention, nothing personal. Unless they make me angry!" My dad joked, clawing at the air.

It was cheesy, but it was your classic dad joke, something I'd been missing in my life up until that point.

"Then, remind me not to cross you."

"You never could, even if you tried, but enough about that, let's move on to the next thing I've got for you," He said, walking toward the exit.

I followed him closely, glancing back once at the information room then turning back ahead. At the prospect of a place just as amazing as the one before, I found myself growing even more excited. The walk there was nearly torture.

We arrived at a large round room that already had several people inside chatting indistinctly. Some of them were humanoid, but lots of them were varying degrees of inhuman. At the sight of my father, they quieted down, leaning back in their chairs to wait for whatever he had to say.

It amazed me to see how much of an effect he had on people, how much they respected him and hoped for his approval. Was this because of his status only, or do they genuinely respect him as a person? Had he earned this respect, or was it merely out of fear, I wonder.

The table in the center of the room was oval in shape, with chairs on either side. At the head, with a window to its back, was an extra-large chair with fancy looking upholstery on the seat. My father pulled a chair up and set it behind and to the right of the head, instructing me to take a seat. He then took his place.

"I know you all have questions, all of which will be addressed, regarding the recent attack on the rebel base, but for now, let's start with Senator D4R14N. You have my attention."

"Your Majesty," The senator says, bowing in his seat. "The attack on the rebel base came out of nowhere and appeared to have been unprompted. What do you say about this?"

My father nodded, adjusting his hands.

"Yes, the attack was performed rather quickly but was not

unprompted. A signal was intercepted that posed a threat on the safety of The Senate, in an attempt to prevent a similar attack, we struck while their ships were still on the ground. The civilians were given enough time to flee only warships were destroyed," He replied.

A fishlike alien made a face, shifting in, I assumed, her seat. Seeing this, my father looked up at her.

"Senator S3LK13, I see your dissatisfaction. Please elaborate," My father said.

"Your majesty, why were the rebels allowed to flee? We should have taken the chance to snuff out The Rebellion."

Again, my father was unphased, simply tapping his thumbs together.

"Yes, I see where you are coming from, but may I remind you that our goal is not to kill the rebels but to bring them back into society. If we kill them all, we would just be proving them right."

The fishlike alien nodded, writing some notes down on her holopad. With that dealt with, the meeting continued.

"Senator N4TH4N, you have the floor."

A skinny looking man with abnormally orange skin sat up, adjusting his glasses, he took a look at his holopad before speaking.

"The current rumor is that the rebel leader M4T1LD4 was present before the attack. Is this true? If so, was she apprehended or killed?"

At the mention of mom's name, several of the senators started to murmur to each other. It was like you'd just called upon the devil. Among the chatter, I caught little snippets like "I thought she was long dead," "where has she been hiding," "is The Rebellion planning a new campaign?" Waving his hand, my father silenced all of it.

"Yes, I am aware of the rumors, but due to the sheer number, I won't be able to address them all individually. The investigation is still going, and I will release an official report tomorrow."

"Is there cause for concern?" Another alien asked.

"Not at all, Senator C4TT13. I can assure you everything is under control, we are merely working to ensure the correct timeline of events and making sure no further measures need to be taken. Should anything change, I will let you all know immediately," Dad replied.

None of the aliens spoke after that. They all nodded in approval, then sat with their hands in front of them. Some of them took notes, but other than that, they remained silently waiting.

"If there is nothing else anyone would like to discuss, then I shall call this meeting adjourned."

With the meeting over the senators dispersed. A few walked over to give their respects to my father before leaving like the rest. They practically tripped over themselves, trying to get his approval.

"Wonderful as always, your Majesty."

"I had no doubts."

"Let us know if there is anything more we can do for you."

It was the typical ass kissery, my father thanked each of them, shook their hands, then waved goodbye. Politicians do the same sort of thing back home; at this point, he was probably used to it. When they were all gone, he turned to me with a big smile.

"That was a meeting of The Senate. Well, a short one, usually they are much longer but this one was just a little information swap. What did you think?" He asked.

"It was really cool. I was impressed with how well you kept

them all under control."

"Simple, if I couldn't do that, I'd have no business running this place. You learn tips and tricks as you go along," My father explained, moving the chair I'd been sitting in back into its place.

"True, but still there's got to be some skill to it," I praised.

Dad led me outside, back into the hallway we'd come from. The guards were still there and fell into place behind us. Having them around made me feel like a celebrity. I half expected to turn a corner and see a group of paparazzi pushing to get a shot of us. It was a bit of an ego boost, back home I was the son of the crazy lady in town, but here, I'm royalty.

It was one hell of an upgrade, but I couldn't shake the feeling of nervousness in my stomach. With notoriety, you find yourself center stage in the public eye. Now when you mess up, it's not just the people around who see it, the whole world is watching at all times, and the world never forgets. Make one mistake and you're back to square one with a public approval rate of zero. At that point, I don't think my heritage would do me any good.

"I've got one more thing for us to do today, then it'll be time for dinner."

"What's that?"

"We're going to go for a walk," My father replied.

"A walk? What's so exciting about that? I walk all the time back home."

"Yes, but you've never gone for a walk here. I want you to see this place, with me. I want you to really get a chance to experience The Senate."

A few more guards walked up and joined the ones already behind us, since we were going outside and all. There were now more than ten of them following us, each with a weapon strapped to their waist.

"Do you go for walks often?" I asked.

"Not very," My dad replied, turning down a hallway then heading down a flight of stairs. "It requires a lot of manpower for protection, so I try to limit it for their sake, but on the other hand, it boosts the people's morale."

After the stairs, we went down a hall until we came upon another elevator. We all squeezed in, and one of the guards pressed the bottom button. From what I could tell, there were well over a hundred glowing buttons on the panel, there could have been more, but I couldn't see around all the guards.

The elevator moved so smoothly. It made me sick. It wasn't like the elevators back home, and the effect it was having on me was drawn out over the long distance we had to travel downward. I nearly jumped for joy when we stopped.

As the elevator doors parted, they revealed a large, sterile-looking lobby with a receptionist's desk, a few chairs, and a few plants sitting by the windows. It looked like something you'd see at a hospital or maybe a large business's head office. There was no personality in the room, so bland and unwelcoming.

When we walked by, the receptionist put away her holopad and bowed. Her name tag said "R4YN4".

The doors to the outside automatically opened as we approached, allowing me to finally get a look at the world beyond the windows. Surprisingly, everything looked pretty similar to how things looked on Earth. The streets were lined with people walking this way and that. Some had small children at their side that pointed in shop windows and tugged on their parent's hands. Besides all the space-age looking floating cars that zipped past, everything was oddly normal. I admired the surroundings until some people nearby recognized my father, then all hell broke loose.

"Your majesty!" They yelled, rushing over to get a chance to speak with him.

They held their hands out to shake his hand, raised their babies up to him, and overall acted like a crazy flash mob. It scared me, so I backed further behind the crowd of bodyguards, but dad seemed unphased. He shook hands closest to him, patted the babies on the head, and waved to everyone who wasn't close enough for him to reach.

"Hello, everyone! Thank you, thank you. It's a pleasure to see you all and an honor to receive your support," He said to the crowd.

"Long live AL1TH1US! Long live The Senate!" The crowd chanted in response, pumping their fists in the air.

There was confidence in their voices, showing just how safe their government made them feel, how much they trusted it, and these were random citizens on the street. I would expect this kind of political support only from people gathered at a rally. If you were to do this same thing back home, there's no way you wouldn't have at least one person in the crowd voicing their detest. Here it seemed that everyone was happy, something governments back home could only dream of accomplishing. It made me wonder even more what mom hated so much about this place.

After shaking a few more hands, patting a few more babies, and waving, my father dispersed the crowd with one sweeping motion of his hand. They all went back about their day, walking off with a renewed pep in their step. With the group gone, my father turned to me with a proud grin.

"One day, they'll all gather like that to celebrate you."

"I doubt it, I don't have that kind of charisma."

"Ah, charisma has nothing to do with it. All you have to do is smile and give them something to look up to when things get scary," He said, taking a few steps forward and starting our walk.

"Does it get scary often around here?" I asked.

"No, no, a lot of times, people just panic when things new or confusing start happening. It takes a moment for us to get all the facts and tell the people what happened. Still, you know how it is, during the following moment of silence rumors start to spread, change in intensity, soon a simple earthquake turns into Armageddon!" He replied, throwing his hands up for emphasis.

"It's the same way back home."

"Yes, you get used to it. I like to see what kind of stories they make it. We like to make bets on what story the people are going to cling to the most," He whispered with a grin.

I laughed, thinking about a group of stuffy old politicians chuckling in a room by themselves as they read different news articles blowing things out of proportion. People tend to overreact when they don't know what's happening, politicians have to understand how to deal with that panic. They can laugh at it in private, sure, but they need to show the people a brave face and let them know everything will be alright.

"Hey, about the report tomorrow, are you going to tell them about me?" I mentioned.

"Absolutely. Just imagine, my son, lost, has finally returned to me. The next ruler of The Senate, here at last!"

"They knew I was lost?"

"Well, no, only a select few even knew you existed. When your mother disappeared I tried to keep it a secret. We were going to announce her pregnancy when we got back, but things didn't go as planned, so I hid it from the public while we tried to find her," He explained.

That didn't match what mom had said at all. She never mentioned any plan before, and why would she be announcing a pregnancy she hadn't wanted?

"What was the plan exactly?" I questioned as some small children ran across the sidewalk in front of us, chasing after a ball.

He didn't seem phased at all. Had he been lying, I would have expected him to flinch and take a moment to come up with an answer, but there was no reaction, only a smooth transition into a response.

"A simple one really, we were going to reveal the truth about The Rebellion, announce her pregnancy, and marry."

"Were you two engaged?"

"Yes. I'd proposed a few months before that."

Great, now I have two conflicting stories. Mom never said anything about a proposal, a plan, any of that. Dad's story is much closer to what The Fallen believe, but it doesn't make sense entirely. How can I tell who's lying? Not wanting to give away my suspicion, I nodded and kept walking.

We went for a substantial walk, maybe two, two, and a half miles. In that span, I got to look at all sorts of shops and restaurants. There was food I didn't recognize in the windows, clothes on mannequins, and jewelry on display. It was all so familiar and yet so foreign at the same time. It left me with an air of malaise, not entirely uncomfortable, but a little disorienting. I'm sure I could get used to it all after a while, but for now, it would just be confusing.

The sun was halfway down when we made it back, painting the sky a lovely shade of purple. I didn't think that much time had passed, but day and night are different here, I suppose.

We went back up the way we came, only this time we went to the dining room. Rosa and Nikki, as well as my mom, were already there. The two girls were chatting happily while my mother sat in her chair with her hands folded in her lap. At the sight of the two of us, she sat up and smiled at me.

"What's wrong, mom?" I asked her.

"Nothing, sweetie, long day is all," She affirmed.

"Oh, well, it's good to see you."

My father and I both took our places, allowing dinner to finally begin. As the chefs brought the food out, I turned to Nikki for conversation.

"Did you notice how dark it was outside?" I asked.

"Yes, due to-" My father began, but Nikki cut him off.

"Due to the extreme tilt of the planet's axis combined with the distance from the local star, nights are much longer in some portions of Malacia and much shorter in others. This disparity in the distribution of light rays allows for a wide variety of crops to be grown on the planet," She recited.

"Sounds like somebody sure learned a lot today," Dad laughed.

"Yes! I mean yes sir! It was amazing. There's so much more I want to learn too. One of the scientists, Mrs. NOR4TTY, said she'd be happy to teach me whatever I want to know as her apprentice! Can you believe that Galileo? A galactic astronomer, no no, the first human galactic astronomer!" Her eyes were practically sparkling.

"Can you fit any more words into your title?"

"Give me a minute. I think I can make it to ten," She joked.

We all laughed, hiding the unease I was feeling. Everything was so comfortable, but there were so many questions burning inside of me. I had to ask, but what was the right way to go about it?

"How did your business go today, ma? What all did you have to get done?" I asked as I took a bite of some vegetable I didn't recognize.

"It went fine, sweetie. My old family home is still standing so today I went out to see how it was. It's a little dusty, but with a little work, I think we can get it back in shape."

"Do you miss the convenience store?"

"A little. It was work, and it kept me busy. What about you? Do you two miss school?"

"No."

"Yes."

Nikki and I answered at the same time, but our answers differed. Her firm "no" was much more sound than my uncertain "yes," and it brought the attention of the table to me. Everyone stopped eating to look at me concerned. My mother, in particular, was pallid with worry, her left hand tapped at the table nervously.

"Let me rephrase that. I don't exactly miss school. I'm just worried is all. I mean we left without a word, the school's probably looking for us by now and Nikki's parents they're probably worried sick. It's going to be a pain to sort that all out when we get back the longer we stay here," I explained.

"That's alright. We can run back to your home, get whatever you need sorted out and come back. I can arrange for it tomorrow after I release the statement, R0 would you get started arranging for a-"

"No, dad!" I interrupted.

Realizing how panicked I sounded, I took a moment to calm myself then continued to speak.

"I mean, I wouldn't want to trouble you right now, you've got a lot going on. We can wait a few days until everything here has settled down after your statement. You're sure to have a lot to deal with after that."

We had agreed that we wouldn't lead them to Earth. I had to come up with some explanation to buy us some time until we could find a way to either go back on our own or prove that The Senate wouldn't do anything to harm Earth. I had hoped for the former, but dad jumped at the idea to take us home, I had to come up with an excuse quickly.

"A-Alright, but don't ever think you're an inconvenience to me. If you asked, I would drop everything to help you, your mother and I both," He replied, taking my mother's hand.

Mom gave me a reassuring smile, but it didn't make me feel any better. One of the two staring back at me was lying, and I still had no idea who it was. We finished the rest of our meal without incident.

When we all parted to go to bed, I pulled Nikki aside for another meeting. The two of us headed back to my room, with me checking over my shoulder to make sure we weren't being followed. Nothing had happened so far to expect anyone was spying on me. Still, I worried my behavior at dinner might change that. Once we were safely inside, I called our meeting to order.

"Alright, what have we learned today?"

"Judging by what all you said at dinner, you learned more than I did," She replied, taking a seat on the bed.

"I certainly learned a lot, but I want you to go first. Yours is likely going to take the most time, so we should get that out of the way first."

"Correct but rude. Anyway, I learned tons about the technology of these people, but if I'm being honest, they treated me like a simpleton. When I talked they listened, but I could see it in their eyes, they thought of me as something primitive. I could tell they were examining me the entire time no matter how much they tried to hide it. When someone puts something inside your ear, you can tell it's not for some 'greeting ritual' or whatever they said it was about. They see humans as beneath them, I'm assuming they only humored me because I'm your friend. I was having the time of my life, but they made me feel like I didn't belong. Is that crazy? Should I just accept it and move on? Live as their subordinate for the rest of my life?" She sighed.

"No, no, you deserve much more than that. Just because we haven't discovered all the stuff they have doesn't make us simple. I'm sure if they gave you a chance, you could discover things that would turn their ideas of the Universe on their heads!" I replied.

"Good pep talk. Now moving on to what you found out today," She said without sitting up.

"Right, I learned some about how the government works around here, but more important than that, my dad is planning on making an announcement tomorrow about catching mom. He said some things that I don't know if I believe."

"Like?"

"Well, he said there was some plan he and mom agreed on, but mom never mentioned anything like that, and why would she have run away if there was a plan involved? Also they were engaged before mom announced her allegiance to The Rebellion, she never mentioned that either. These stories aren't adding up, and I don't know what to do," I groaned, flopping face-first onto the bed beside her.

"Indeed. Hey nice save at dinner by the way. I know I wasn't much help, but I couldn't think of a good excuse either."

"It's alright. I figured something out."

"You always do, just like you're going to with this whole thing with your parents. I trust you'll think of something, and if not, I'm right here to bail you out."

"I know, but this isn't another astronomy test I didn't study for. This is my entire life we're talking about."

"Yes, but if you think about it, this is just another test you didn't study for. You're either going to pass or fail, and hopefully that won't make you fail the class called life," She said, her eyes sparkling as she threw her hands outward.

"Nikki, promise me you'll never be a motivational speaker."

"Was it really that bad? I had this whole other bit planned."

"Oh, hush!" I laughed, hitting her with a pillow.

"Who takes long now, huh?" She replied, grabbing another pillow to fight back with.

It was childish, but I needed it. Having that silly pillow fight put me at ease and made me feel ready for whatever tomorrow had to throw at me.

Once we'd given each other a thorough thrashing, I walked her to the door. She stepped outside and waved goodbye, but before she could disappear around the corner, I fired off one of the new insults I had thought up.

"Goodnight, Neanderthal."

"Sleep tight troglodyte."

Shit hers rhymed. While I sleep, I'm going to have to think up something even better. That'll distract me from the fact that tomorrow I'm going to hopefully learn the truth and probably start some drama.

11

Chapter 11

I loved the sound of that chime. It made me feel so important every time it went off. I always jumped up with joy and ran over to let the machine do my hair. My poofs had never been this perfect before, not even when my mom did them.

Once I'd brushed my teeth, the door to my room opened.

"Good morning Nikki, are you ready for today?" Rosalina asked, surprisingly, without having to put away her holopad.

"I am, I am, are the others coming?"

"Not today, I thought I would treat you to something special," Rosalina answered.

"Oh? Like what?"

"I figured you'd like to check out our on-site science lab."

"You figured correctly," I laughed.

After running back to grab my phone, I gestured for her to lead the way. She nodded, turning and walking in the direction of the lab. It was a pleasant walk, little further than to the dining room, taking me down all sorts of hallways, both familiar and not.

Every time they take me somewhere new around here, I'm always surprised. The entryways all look the same, so I never know what lies within. Back home, we would label things or use different doors for different rooms, so you could at least tell which ones were more important. None of the bedrooms had any personality, either. My room had a massive poster from my favorite space movie on it, letting anyone who approached know it belonged to me and what I was into.

"Here we are," Rosalina said, stopping at a door that looked no different from the others.

When she opened the door, the strong chemical smell of cleaner hit my nose, making it scrunch up. Even though I hated the scent, I couldn't stop myself from gasping in shock, sucking even more of it into me.

The lab was incredible. It was bigger than two typical classrooms put together, plenty of room for all sorts of equipment. Beakers, flasks, and test tubes filled with liquids of every color sat on countertops, just begging to be fiddled with. There were other containers too, but their shapes weren't like anything we had on Earth.

Everywhere aliens who wore lab coats over their bodysuits weaved in and out, moving things, mixing, and prodding. Most of them ignored our arrival, except for a female alien with shiny bluish skin. She turned to us and smiled, setting down what she'd been working on.

"Hello, R0S4L1N4!" She chirped, running over and shaking her hand.

"Hello, Dr. F41TH3."

"And you must be the Earthling!" The scientists said.

She reached out and shook my hand vigorously, one of those handshakes that makes you think your hand is going to pop out

135

of place.

"Hi, My name's Nikki," I said.

"Ni-kki, intriguing. How did you get your name?"

"My parents gave it to me. I think it was my mom that suggested it," I replied.

"What does it mean?"

"I don't think it has a meaning."

"Really? How archaic."

The scientist, Dr. Faithe, pulled an otoscope from one of the pockets in her jacket and held it up to my ear. It was cold, making me wince. I gave her a confused look as she shifted to check the other ear.

"Oh, sorry, dear, this is just a greeting ceremony. No reason to be alarmed," She lied.

It hurt a little, being treated like I wouldn't understand what was happening. Did she think we don't have doctors or scientists? Maybe she was worried it would scare me if I knew I was being examined.

Putting aside the otoscope, she moved on to a tongue depressor.

"Open wide," She instructed.

She placed the depressor in my mouth and turned on a light on her head. Directing my tongue out of her way, she examined every inch of my mouth. I thought she was going to stick her head inside; she was so thorough.

"31, 32, 33 teeth. About the same as Vaads," Faithe commented.

That reminded me, I had a wisdom tooth that had come through the gum. The other three were still under. I was supposed to have them all removed, but I postponed the surgery for school.

"Wait, most humans don't have this many teeth. I've got what we call a 'wisdom' tooth. I've got to have it removed," I explained.

"So, humans have 32 teeth?"

"Yes, ma'am, as adults."

"Does the number change?"

"Yes, as babies, we only have 20."

"Weird. What's the advantage in that?" She wondered aloud.

On her holopad, she made a note of what all I had told her. After she put it away, she got up and brought over a microscope. She quickly grabbed a strand of my hair and pulled it out, placing it on a slide then slipping it on the stage.

She pushed a button on the side and the scope autofocused. I couldn't believe it. I thought for sure she'd have to further adjust it, but when she put her eye up to the lens, she exclaimed with interest.

"R0S4, come take a look at this," She said.

Rosalina put away her holopad and walked over to get a look.

"Let's see. Slightly oval in shape, the thickest portion is," She pushed another button on the side. "60 microns."

"Let me see," Rosalina said.

"Here, let's check the database."

Faithe stepped aside and let Rosalina look into the microscope while she fiddled with her holopad. Once she pulled up what she wanted, she tapped Rosalina and gently pushed her aside.

"Here, I'll read the information out to you, then you enter it into the database and see if we get any matches."

"Yes, ma'am," Rosalina replied, taking the holopad.

While they worked on that, I looked around the room for something to occupy myself with. There were all sorts of interesting things lying around, but I didn't trust myself not to mess anything up, until my eyes came upon a computer. It was sitting on the corner of the table, with its screen already booted up. After a quick glance at the ladies, I slowly walked over to it.

When I touched the screen, it brought me to a menu labeled "Access database" with hundreds of names on it. I didn't understand why a scientist would even have this sort of thing. Oh, wait, duh, she probably can control who has access to the lab.

After another glance their way, I started scrolling through the names, looking for one in particular.

"The shape of the medulla is closest to those from planet J'Lambda."

"Good, now let's look at the distribution of melanin," I heard Faith say, letting me know they were still busy.

After lots of scrolling, I finally found it, Galileo's file. I copied the file and renamed it "Nikki," then I reset the hand scan. The computer prompted me to put my hand up against a specified portion of the screen with a green border. When I touched it, the area under my hand glowed. A few moments later, a little message popped up that "handprint confirmed". Mission accomplished.

I slid back over to the other two and pretended I was paying deep attention. On the holopad was a 3d model of a strand of hair similar to my own. Its stats were next to it, and they matched everything Faithe had mentioned.

"Alright, now let's file that under human," Faithe said, taking the holopad back.

Once she was done, she slid her chair over to me, an excited grin on her face as she looked at me.

"Would you be opposed to me taking a blood sample? It's part of the ritual."

"Uh, I wouldn't mind."

"Lovely, I'll make sure to get that before you leave, but for now, I'd like to talk to you about your planet. What is your solar system like?"

"Well, we've got one major star, we call it the sun, and around it orbits 8 planets and several smaller bodies."

"What is the size of your sun?"

"Excuse me?"

"Oh, sorry, your sun is how many light-years in diameter?"

I had completely forgotten that one. Usually, when we talk about the size of stars in astronomy, we refer to them as being a certain number of suns large, which communicates its size relatively. That was always good enough for my purposes, but I didn't remember what it really meant. Kind of like using instead of 3.14, it made the math more manageable, but you don't really get to see the scope of what you're talking about. I mean, 4 seems smaller than 12.56, but in reality, it's the opposite.

"It's 860,000 something miles wide."

"Miles? Could you put that in terms of light-years?"

"Uh, I'm not sure I can do that math."

"Alright, can you do the opposite? How many miles is a light-year?"

"5.88 Trillion."

"I can work with that," Faithe said, using her holopad to do some math.

It took her a while, but eventually, she had her number, which she put in the same note that she had about me. Then she pulled up a photo of a star similar to the sun, the same phase, and everything.

"Like this?"

"Yeah! That's pretty close."

She pushed another button, and a much larger, blue star appeared next to it. It dwarfed the sun, making it look like a beetle.

"Here's the star Malacia orbits. It is a blue supergiant we call, Amadeus."

"Wow. It's beautiful. How do you guys even have a night?" I asked.

"That's because of the extreme tilt of the planet. It's actually beneficial, creates a wide range of climates."

"That's amazing."

"So you said Earth is where the Earthling's originated from, but how many planets do they currently have under their control?"

"Only the one."

She stopped typing to give me a shocked look.

"Is that weird?"

"Yeah, a little, an intelligent species with only one planet under their control. It's….… forget I said anything. Would you like to watch us work on some new nanites?" She said, trying to save the moment.

"Sure."

Experiments revolving around the nanites took up over half of the lab, and 3/4ths of the scientists. They were in beakers being heated, test tubes being magnetized, and on Petri dishes with strangely colored bacteria.

In one large test tube, a disembodied ear was being rebuilt by nanites. Once it was complete, a scientist pulled it out, cut it in half, and put each half in a different tube, allowing the process to restart.

"The donor organs are looking incredible, M1K3."

"Thank you, F4. I suspect we'll be able to start rolling these out within the next few months," The scientist replied.

"Why would people need these if the nanites can grow things back?" I asked.

"It's for people who were born missing something or who were injured before the nanites were injected into them. In those cases, the nanites don't do any regrowing, so we have to attach a donor organ that can graft to the patient," The male scientist explained.

His explanation blew me away. I hadn't thought about that before. It would be kind of weird if a kid who was born without a leg suddenly had one burst from the point where it would have been. If someone lost an ear years ago and it had already healed, it'd be terrifying if one suddenly burst out of the scar tissue.

The other experiments in the lab were all just as amazing. If something like this was happening on Earth, countries would fight over who would have the rights to it. I can't even begin to imagine how many trillions of funding it would take.

All the scientists when they met me went into full examination mode, poking and prodding all over. Faithe still tried to say it was a greeting. Thankfully they stopped if I ever voiced my discomfort.

"My apologies. We should have taken into consideration how unfamiliar you are with our customs. Forgive me," One of them said, bowing.

I didn't really care, but he was making such a big deal of it. It almost made me feel guilty for saying anything. Faithe tried to take my mind off it by explaining more of their experiments while someone was looking at me, but it didn't work.

On the one hand, I was thrilled to be in the presence of such advanced scientific innovation, but on the other, it made me feel like a child. While on Earth, I could talk about astronomy with the best of them, but here I knew less than the least informed citizens. It was a significant blow to my ego, but I guess I should have seen it coming.

It was naive of me to think I could have kept up with aliens. I should have guessed they'd be far more advanced than humans, or was it that I wanted to impress them?

I had always imagined they'd pick me up in their ship, and we'd talk about all sorts of cool things, with me teaching them. They would say something like, "Wow! You're so smart. How do humans know all of this?" and I'd help them solve problems and build things.

Of course, if they had mastered space travel, there's no way I would have been able to keep up with them. I'm so stupid, I should have realized this ages ago, all I did was get my hopes up.

"Is something wrong?" Rosalina asked when she noticed me spacing out.

"No, I'm fine, just thinking about stuff. I'm getting a little homesick," I lied.

Is it because I wanted attention? Am I one of those kids who seek attention from others because I lack it at home? Am I just repeating things I've read online? Absolutely.

"I'm impressed with how quickly you're picking all of this up. I thought for sure it'd be too much for you," Faithe praised, knocking me out of my internal crisis.

"You think so? I'm not going to lie, it is pretty mind-blowing," I admitted.

"Don't sell yourself short. When R0S4 gave me a quick explanation about the situation, I was so sure I'd be explaining every word to you, but you're special. I imagine back on Earth you're quite a little genius," She complimented.

"You really think so?"

"Trust me, I'm a good judge of character. I'm sure if you worked with me, you'd catch up to us with no time."

"You really think so?"

"Yes, enough for me to offer you an internship."

"Wait, really?"

My entire body nearly folded like a piece of paper from excitement at the prospect of being a scientist's intern in space. I had always planned to intern with someone brilliant, and I'd hoped my parent's connections could hook me up with someone, but this was far better than anything they could have worked out.

"I'd love to have you. It warms my heart to see young people so enthralled by science. It'd be an honor to foster that excitement," She assured me.

In the back of my head, I knew she was only saying this to get on my good side. That's why all of them were being so nice to me. Being friends with the king's son sure does have its perks.

"When would I be able to start?"

"Whenever you can. If you want, I'm starting a new series of testing for a new and improved fabric in a month or so. You could wait till then and start with that."

"That sounds fantastic. I would love to."

"Great. It's a plan, now let's get that blood sample."

She took three whole vials before letting me go. I usually despise having blood drawn, but with their super-advanced needles, I didn't feel a thing, not even a tiny pinprick. If the needles were like this back home, I'd give blood more often.

When she finished, Rosalina led me out toward the dining room for dinner.

"That was amazing, girl, we have to do that again sometime."
"Perhaps if we have time," She replied, without looking at me.

12

Chapter 12

The morning followed just like the ones before. The chime woke me up, and my clothes were presented to me, although this time they were far fancier. It wasn't just a skin-tight bodysuit this time; now it had shoulder pads, a cape, and some other bangles.

All the added ornaments made it hard for me to get into it. Things didn't quite sit right, and the shoulder pads looked crooked. Ignoring that for now, I went about the rest of my routine. Once I was done, the door opened.

"Good morning Galileo!" My father called in a sing-song voice.

"Good morning, dad," I replied, exiting the bathroom into the main room.

Dad was dressed in the same sort of over the top getup, but his was even more so. Mine had silver accents while his were that same weird rainbow metal everything's made of. When he saw how I looked, he made a sweet face and walked over.

"Oh, son, you're so…. crooked," He laughed, fixing my shoulder pads.

"Sorry, I've never had to wear anything this fancy before," I admitted.

"You did good for a first try I'd say. They're at least kind of in the right spot."

I laughed and rolled my eyes, knowing he was just being nice. Thinking about this reminded me a lot of a father fixing his son's tie like I see on tv all the time. Back home, I never had many chances to wear a tie, and whenever I did, mom tried her best to figure it out, but she never did get it right.

"I'm glad they fit. I told your roommate you'd be needing something formal last night, I'm glad it was able to whip up something."

"My roommate?" I asked as he backed away to make sure everything was in place.

"Yes, the robot inside your room. That's what we call them. Remarkable, aren't they? They make life so much easier," He replied.

With one final adjustment, Dad backed away and admired his work. He sighed happily and held his hands together, looking me up and down. A tear seemed to form in the corner of his eyes.

"Is something wrong?"

"No, I'm just... so happy. I'm so happy you exist," He wiped his eyes. "Let's get going, this announcement isn't going to make itself."

The guards greeted us at the door and fell into place behind us like usual. I had grown more used to it at this point. In the future, I hoped to learn their names so I could actually get to know them. It would be nice to have a relationship with the people who protect me, it would make me feel safer.

Before we got to the elevator, Rosalina joined us, her face

buried in her holopad like usual. She gave me a quick "good morning" before taking her place among us.

"Where's Nikki?" I asked her.

"I figured she wouldn't want to deal with getting dressed up for something she's not really involved in. She'll be joining us later," She stated.

"Oh," I sighed.

I had wanted her to be there with me today, but I understand. This is a lot of work for something she's only a bystander to. She can just skip all the hard stuff and get back with us once that's done.

Looking down, I realized Rosalina was wearing some beautiful clothes too. Her's weren't as fancy as mine, but they were clearly of the higher end of clothing. The main bodysuit she wore was silver with the slightest hint of pink that really brought out the color in her eyes. She wore no shoulder pads, but she did have a very charming and ornate cape that attached to her collar and hung loosely on her back. When she walked, it bounced, catching the light in a dazzling display of color.

We all filed into the elevator one at a time, starting with two guards, so my father, Rosalina, and I ended up surrounded. One of them near the door hit the top button, and we started moving upward.

"Galileo," My dad said, breaking the silence.

"Yes?"

"I want you to know that everything I say today may not make a lot of sense to you, you've only ever had your mother's side of the story, so it's going to be startling to hear the truth. Can you promise me you'll listen?" He said.

I paused, thinking it over for a moment. He was so severe, he looked at me, and I could see the gravity of the situation evident on his face.

"I-I promise."

"Good."

With that, he turned forward and stood up straight, preparing himself to face his people.

I thought initially that my father's office was the highest you could go, but the elevator took us to the roof of the building. It was still dark outside, but I could see fresh slivers of light just starting to creep over the horizon. There were hundreds of floating platforms surrounding us, all aimed at the podium at the edge of the building.

Thousands of aliens stared back at us. Ones with nice-looking clothing sat on platforms higher up while others with lower end clothes stood on ones crowded below. There were also ships hovering in place to watch the announcement. For those who couldn't be in attendance, dozens of cameras floated around, capturing every angle possible.

When the elevator doors opened, a tremendous uproar of cheer spread through the crowd. It sounded like the loudest football game you could imagine. They began to chant his name as he approached the podium, arms up in approval.

"AL1! AL1! AL1!"

Raising one hand, he silenced them all. Rosalina and I took our places behind him, and behind us, the guards formed into a tight line with their hands folded in front of them. The people held their breath, the cameras moved for the best angle, and everyone craned to get a chance to hear this important announcement.

"Thank you all for coming, I know there's been a lot going on lately, and you all have many questions, I will do my best to assuage you all and explain what happened," He began.

"Recently, The Senate, per my command, launched an attack on the previously peaceful base of the Fallen, one of the last hideouts of The Rebellion. This attack was not unprompted, as many of you have guessed, we had reason to believe that The Rebellion leader M4T1LD4 had been brought in for questioning."

At the mention of mom's name, the crowd began to mutter and stir. Some grabbed their children in fear, others closed their eyes as horrible memories racked their mind, it was clear that everyone in the crowd had been affected by her in some way. After giving them all a moment to calm down, dad continued.

"M4 was apprehended and brought into our custody. The remaining members fled, and their base was destroyed in an attempt to prevent a resurgence in rebellion activity."

His explanation brought the people comfort. Knowing mom was behind bars instead of running free made them feel safer, but now they had new questions. I'm sure they all wanted her head by the way they glared. They wanted her blood in repayment for the lives lost fighting the war she started, I could see it in their eyes. It terrified me.

"However, moving forward, there is something you all should know."

The crowd perked up.

"M4 was not acting on her own. Several solar years ago, before the start of The Rebellion, M4 confided in me that she suspected there was a rebellion brewing in The Senate's military. As general, she had insider insight and had caught wind of a plot to overthrow the government. The two of us formed a plan to prevent this Rebellion from ever getting off the ground and to keep them from causing any lasting damage. She acted as my spy, pretending to lead The Rebellion to victory while, in reality, she was running them in circles, throwing them off and exposing disobedient members of society. The culmination of this plan went perfectly. The battle at the Omega Quaser ended, permanently crippling The Rebellion's militia, and M4 was retrieved. We then proceeded to take out as many unprotected rebel bases as we could on our way back to Malacia. However, during this time, we discovered she was pregnant with my child. As her due date approached, I suggested she leave me with a map of the bases and head to Arrowyn for the delivery. The two of us planned to return to Malacia to announce the results of her espionage and our child's birth, but while she was traveling, a strong solar storm knocked her off course. She ended up getting sucked through a jump and crash landing on a planet several light-years beyond our known universe. Fearing her dead, I chose to keep her disappearance a secret as well as her espionage, and allow everyone to believe she had died to prevent widespread panic."

He turned back to me with a reassuring grin before continuing.

"Thanks to some miracle, M4 was recovered as well as our child. My son, Galileo, has finally returned to me, to us. It is an honor to introduce to you all the future king of The Senate, my heir," He said, gesturing for me to come forward.

As I walked up, the crowd cheered for me like I was some sort of celebrity. They chanted my name, waved things in the air, clapped vigorously, throwing themselves into the celebration. I tried to keep a brave face for them, but on the inside, my mind felt like it was turning to jelly.

Dad's explanation was both believable and not. I wanted to believe it, wanted this all to disappear, and we could finally start living as a family, but things weren't adding up. Mom said she gave birth to me after being pregnant for five months, three of which were spent on the ship, why would she have gone to Arrowyn that Early? I didn't believe him, but I knew I couldn't make a scene and scare all the citizens.

A few reporters floated up on small platforms and asked us questions, more him than me. They pointed their microphones and read questions from their holopads, annotating the answers, then slowly hovering away to let the next one in line to take their place.

Once we'd answered maybe 20 reporters, my father raised his hand and announced that the report was over. They all cheered once again as we made the walk back to the elevator. When the doors were closed, I couldn't hold in my anger anymore. I had to get to the truth, even if it meant making things uncomfortable.

"Why did you lie?" I asked.

Rosalina shifted in place, my father looked at me, shocked.

"What do you mean? I told the truth, it may be different from what your mother said but-"

"Dad, that doesn't even make sense. Maybe to the citizens it does but not to me, I know more than you think I do!" I cut him off.

"Galileo! Do not raise your voice at me. I know you're confused, but now is not the time for us to be fighting. Let's just calm down, and we can talk things through, I'll explain everything you want to know."

"What about mom? I want to talk to her too. I want to know what she has to say about your explanation, why the two don't align."

"That's fine son, at dinner we'll-"

"No, I want to go see her now!"

The doors to the elevator opened just as I yelled, allowing

151

anyone nearby to hear. Nikki was standing there looking excited, but her face dropped when she heard me.

"It seems like a bad time I'll just get out of here."

"No, Nikki. I want you with me. I want us all to go see mom right now!" I demanded.

We all stepped out of the elevator and regrouped. Dad was looking down at me, frustrated with Rosalina right behind. I met his glare head-on with my arms crossed, Nikki did the same behind me. She didn't know what this fight was about, but she sided with me anyway.

"Alright, son, give me one moment to find out where she is," He said, pulling out his holopad.

He started dialing some number, but I grabbed his hand to stop him.

"No calling people. I want to surprise her."

This would be the real test. If my mother wasn't warned about us coming, then my father couldn't control her. He couldn't move her somewhere that fit his narrative and threaten her to act a certain way.

"And why is that?" He growled.

"Why is that such a big deal?"

"She could be busy, we wouldn't want to interrupt her."

"Fine, if she's busy, take me to where she is so I can see her being busy, then we'll just leave."

"Son, you're being ridiculous."

"I am not! Unless you've got something to hide, this shouldn't be a problem." I said, finally cluing him in to my suspicions.

I didn't care anymore about avoiding a fight, I needed to know what was going on around here, and his behavior just made me suspect him even more. Finally, he sighed, rubbing the space between his brows.

"Alright, I'll take you to see her. She told me yesterday where she would be, let's just hope she isn't busy," He relented.

In a huff, he turned and began to lead the way. It was clear he was angry, his face said it all, maybe he thought I wasn't looking because he wasn't hiding it at all. His hands were by his sides, swinging with his arms, but I noticed him making fists around his thumbs, something he doesn't normally do.

The walk to mom took us down several flights of stairs, an elevator trip, and down long hallways to places I hadn't been before. It seemed darker than usual. There were no windows to allow me to see outside, so the only light was from the bulbs overhead.

We finally came to a stop outside of a bleak metal door.

"Before we go in, I should find out if she's bus-" My father began, but before he could come up with another excuse, I reached up and hit the panel to open the door.

The two metal panels slid apart, revealing a large room with a tall ceiling. It was round in shape, with walls made of what I guessed were one-way windows for observation, and at the center was my mother strapped to some sort of table in an upright position. Her restraints were glowing, just like the ones they used on her during the trial at the Fallen's base. Her eyes went wide when she noticed us.

"Galileo!" She cried.

"Mom!"

I ran to her side, trying to see how I could free her. All I could think of was getting her out, adrenaline pumping through me as I examined the contraption keeping her in place. In my panic, I had almost forgotten my father was still there, but the booming sound of his voice reminded me.

"Damnit, son! Get away from your mother."

"Why is she restrained? You said she was on your side!" I yelled.

"Son, listen to me."

"No! I'm done listening to you, you've done nothing but lie to me!"

I found a panel on the back of the table, removing it revealed a button, and when I pressed it, the blue rings holding mom in place disappeared. She stood up and stepped away from the table, immediately moving to get between my father and me.

"You're so much like your mother! You couldn't just leave things be."

Nikki stood to the side, trying to stay out of the way. She was observing everything, ready to step in if needed.

"Tell me the truth. I've already caught you lying; you might as well just tell me. Otherwise, mom will," I threatened.

He paused and looked between the two of us thoughtfully. The gears in his head were turning as he tried to come up with a way out of this, you could almost hear them grinding, but he knew he had to relent, he was caught, and there was no way out.

"Alright, you want the truth? Here's the truth! Your mother did start a rebellion against me; she never was on my side. I abducted her after the battle of the Omega Quasar and gave her an out."

"A what?"

Dad walked towards us threateningly, like a predator chasing prey. He circled us, forcing mom to match his movements to stay between us.

"An out. After what she did, the entirety of The Senate wanted her head on a pike. I tried to save her!"

"Oh, don't act like you did me some service by getting me

pregnant."

"Silence, M4. I told your mother the risk, told her how the people would want her dead, and explained my plan to her. If she had just followed it like she was supposed to, we wouldn't be in this mess."

"What plan?"

"I planned to tell The Senate she had been working for me the entire time, like I did today. Then we could announce her pregnancy, another layer of protection for her since the people wouldn't want to kill the mother of my heir, then she would have given birth to you on Arrowyn. Her mistake would have just disappeared, but she ruined it by running away!"

"That's why you changed the story, isn't it?"

"That's right, son. Your mother did run away, that's why the timeline didn't match up, but the only way you could have known is if you remembered the series of events that your mother had explained to you. I have to say, I am both beyond angry with you, and extremely proud. You're smarter than you appear," My dad explained.

"Shut up, AL. Our son is brilliant, it was your own mistake for underestimating him," My mom defended me.

"This was all your fault, M4!" Another voice broke through, this time it was Rosalina.

She finally had her face out of her holopad. Her cheeks were red, and her fists were clenched so tight they shook.

"Excuse me? You stay out of this, you have no right to talk about matters you know nothing about."

"Yes, I do! You killed my father for your stupid war. AL was kind enough to spare you from death, which if you ask me, was too good for you. You should have been grateful."

Mom looked at her with a mixture of anger and intrigue. She

approached her slowly, tilting her head to get a better look at her. Even though they had met before, mom didn't know much about her.

"I know you. You're L3L4ND's child, aren't you? You have no idea what he was like. I killed him because he was a sorry, no good, monstrous bastard of a man who had no right to even be in his position-"

Before mom could finish her rant, Rosalina reached into her pocket and pulled out a ray gun. She brandished it with incredible speed, firing before anyone could even attempt to stop her, sending a bolt of plasma right into mom's head. Instantly, mom went from standing in front of her to laying headless on the floor, nothing but a burnt stub left. My voice caught in my throat, my legs nearly fell out from under me, all I could do was fall to the ground and cradle her body as I screamed in anguish.

"Ms.M!" Nikki yelled, rushing over to join me.

We were both in tears, cradling mom's body as if it would bring her back. A ringing sound filled my ears, barely audible over my own wails. The feeling of her body in my hands felt so surreal, like a dream almost, but I knew I was awake, I could tell by the sensation of her body heat against my skin.

When I looked over at Dad, he was standing next to Rosalina, scolding her like a child. He had taken the blaster from her and was holding it in his hand.

"What have I told you about shooting this thing inside? Just look at the mess you made, someone is going to have to clean this up, you know."

They were both acting so calmly, so normal. I wanted to hurt them for ignoring my pain. It didn't make sense to me how they could be so calm right after my mother was killed. I went to yell at them, but then I noticed some movement in mom.

Where her neck had been, the burn began to disappear, replaced with healthy skin cells that slowly crept upward, forming the missing part of her neck. They continued up further, forming her chin, then the rest of her head. I could see the bones developing first, being covered by muscle, then the skin sealed it all up. It worked it's way up, finishing with her hair. Her eyes were closed at first, and she didn't move, then suddenly she sat up with a gasp.

With wild eyes, she took several deep frantic breaths keeping her hand over her heart like she was trying to feel her own heartbeat. I was still in such shock, but I couldn't resist the sudden urge to hug her.

"What was that? Did- Did I die?" She asked between gasps.

"Those were the nanites darling. They can repair any part of you as long as there is something left to work from, you'd know all about them if you hadn't run away," My father sneered.

"You're a monster! I want to go home, I'm taking mom, and we're leaving, I never should have come here in the first place," I said, helping mom to her feet.

"You're making this harder on yourself, son. You three aren't going anywhere."

With a snap of his fingers, guards came in, grabbing Nikki and I. They wrenched us away from my mom, who my father dealt with. He grabbed her wrists and slammed her against the table, hitting the button to turn the restraints back on with his knee.

The guards dragged us, kicking and screaming out the room. Once we were back to the level our bedrooms were on, the guards split off, taking Nikki to hers and me to mine. My father stayed with that group. They threw me into my room, sending me to the floor. I quickly regained my footing and stood up to face them, but now it was only my father and I in the room. He stood, blocking the doorway, looking down at me like I was a bug under his foot.

"Our first fight, how adorable," He teased.

"You won't get away with this. I'll expose you to the universe. I will never be your heir."

"I see you've got a lot of emotions to work out. Until you come to your senses, you'll be spending some time in here."

"Like hell, I will!" I yelled, rushing forward and attempting to push him from my doorway.

My push did nothing, bouncing off of him like it was nothing. It felt like I'd run into a brick wall, and not to toot my own horn, but I'm stronger than most kids my age. I gulped when I realized my mistake.

"Your mother really did you a disservice, she left you weak," He pushed me back into the room, sending me back onto the floor. "You can come out of your room when you are ready to be a good son."

With that, he stepped back and allowed the doors to shut. I ran up to them and tried to hit the panel to make them open, but they wouldn't budge. An error message popped up whenever I put my hand on it, meaning he'd disabled my handprint. Correction, Rosalina disabled my handprint, that techy know it all.

I beat on the doors until my hands were sore, I tried to pry them open with no luck, I threw whatever I could find at them anything I could think of to try and get out. I kept trying until my muscles ached, finally giving in to my fatigue. My room was a mess, but I didn't care. I ran over to the bed and slammed my face into the mattress, then screaming until my throat hurt.

I wish we'd never come to space, that Nikki never intercepted that transmission, that mom had kept her true identity a secret forever. Of all the miserable things to happen, this would have to be one of the worst possible.

There was nothing for me to do. I couldn't sleep, couldn't play on my phone since it died a while ago, couldn't read a book, all I could do was stare up at the ceiling angrily. If I had mind powers, my anger would be so intense that it would destroy the lightbulb above me. It would shatter into a million pieces and rain down on me, another casualty to my destructive outburst. Maybe the noise would alert someone, and they'd come get me. I could take a piece of glass and cut my hand then scream for medical attention. Using that as an opening, I could slip out and escape, grabbing my mother on the way, but I don't have mind powers, so that stupid bulb was safe.

After running through several escape scenarios, all of which sounded fantastic up until a point, I was alerted to a noise at my door. It slid open and someone quickly stepped inside, allowing it to close behind them. I got up, expecting it to be someone coming to punish me, but when they turned around, I realized it was Nikki.

"Nikki!" I yelled, running over and hugging her.

"What have I said about hugging?" She joked.

"Wait," I said, pushing her away. "How'd you get in here? All of my accesses have been revoked."

"They don't know I'm in the system. I used the computer in the lab to add myself when they weren't paying attention," She explained.

"You're a genius."

"That's right. Let's go get your mom and the others."

Taking her hand, we rushed out the door, looking left and right to check for guards before rushing off towards where my

159

mother was being held.

13

Chapter 13

We managed to slip past dozens of guards on our way down to the holding cells. There were a few close calls where we opted to take the stairs instead of an elevator to avoid suspicion. By the time we made it down to that level, we'd done so much running around our legs were hurting.

"Ok, we know what room mom's in, but what about her friends?" I whispered.

"All the empty rooms have green wall panels, but occupied ones have red. The only other red one I saw was down the hall from your mom."

"That's got to be them. Let's get them first, they shouldn't have as much security as mom," I suggested.

"Good idea."

After checking to make sure the coast was clear, we snuck over to the other occupied room. While I kept watch, Nikki opened the door. We looked inside real quick to make sure it was the right room, then hopped inside to stay hidden.

"Galileo, Nikki." Juliet cried out with joy.

The others perked up when they heard her, smiling when they saw it was really us. They, too, were held against tables like the one holding mom, but their room didn't have the one-way windows.

"Are guys ok?" I asked.

Mom was allowed out to see us at dinner, but there was no telling how long the three of them had gone without moving.

"We're fine, what about you two?" L14NG replied.

"We're perfect. Here let's get you guys out of there." I said, walking over to L14NG and pushing the button to remove him.

One by one, I released them, finally letting them stretch. They were a bit wobbly on their legs at first, but they got the hang of it and were standing proud once again. The five of us gathered around to figure out a plan. We explained the situation to them up until that point. They listened carefully, nodding, and rubbing their chins in thought.

"Alright, we need to get M4 and get you kids, out of here. Retrieving M4 is the easy part, but once we've got her, it'll be hard to get to the launch pad without incident. Are either of you armed?" Juliet asked.

"No," Nikki and I replied dejectedly.

"That's alright. It would have helped, but we can do without. That means we can't take any chances here," Juliet said.

"JUL13T, you take the kids and go get M4. L14NG and I will cause a distraction and buy you guys enough time to get to the hanger," BR16S spoke up.

"No, you two shouldn't; it's too dangerous."

"Don't worry, JU. It'd be more of a hassle than anything for them to kill us with these new nanites. We'll distract them long enough for you guys to get out of here," L14NG reassured her.

"I know, but it's not fair."

"Ah, come on, it's only gentlemanly for us to. It is the men's job to protect the women and children after all," L14NG joked, sticking his tongue out.

Juliet laughed and punched him on the arm. They laughed, but a moment later, Juliet gave the two of them tight hugs, wishing them luck. After taking a breather, we split up.

The two men ran down the hall, staying quiet until they were far enough away from us, while the three of us shuffled over to mom's room. Nikki opened the door for us, allowing us to slip in before she let it close.

"Guys!" Mom whisper yelled.

We ran over and freed her as quickly as we could. As her feet hit the ground, an alarm began to sound off in the distance.

"We've gotta go," Juliet warned.

Mom nodded, following us out the door without a moment's hesitation. Although it had been a while since we'd been to the hanger, Nikki seemed to remember the way correctly. It made sense, she was probably preparing in case this all went south from the beginning.

When we got there, only ships filled the massive room. All the soldiers were probably either asleep or dealing with the issues BR16S and L14NG were causing.

"Now, which of these ships can get us out of here," Juliet wondered out loud.

Mom grabbed a spare piece of metal and was about to smash the control panel on a nearby ship, but I stopped her in time.

"Mom! We can just take the ship dad gave me," I suggested.

"Right," She replied, dropping the metal with a thud.

We hurried over to the Assayer. Nikki opened the door and invited everyone in. Mom went first, then Juliet, then Nikki, then me last. As I went to step inside, someone grabbed my arm and pulled me back.

"You aren't getting out of here that easily!" My father yelled, pulling as hard as he could on me.

My right foot was still in the door, but I was having a hard time keeping it there. Nikki tried to run over to help me, but I waved her off.

"Get off of me!"

With one quick twist of my body, I punched him square in the nose, breaking the bone. He fell back with a yell, clutching his broken feature in pain. Seizing my chance, I jumped completely inside and closed the door.

"We've got to go right now!" I yelled, holding the button to keep the door shut.

Mom was at the head pushing buttons on the panel, when she hit the right one, the engine came to life with a roar. She grabbed the throttle and eased it forward, jerking the ship upward but not as bad as I did when I first flew it.

"Man, this baby can move," She commented.

With us now off the ground, I joined the rest of them at the head of the ship. I could see my father standing below us, shouting at some approaching soldiers. They then raised their blasters and shot at us, hitting the side and causing warning alarms to sound. Mom seemed unphased, slowly easing the ship forward and out of the hanger.

"We've got to make the jump now!"

"Not yet. They'll follow us," Mom replied.

She turned the ship around, aiming it at the hanger. Many of the people inside were already ahead of her and were running for cover. With a touch of a green button, she blasted the hanger, obliterating many of the ships parked there.

"Now we can go," Mom laughed.

She turned the ship around as the three of us found our seats and strapped in. After making sure we were all seated, she floored it, sending us flying out into space. The alarms were still sounding but the ship appeared to be moving just fine.

"We've got to stop for repairs, one of the thrusters is damaged," Mom announced.

"They won't last till we get to Earth?" Nikki asked.

"No, it's not a big deal now, but the more stress we continue to put on it, the worse it'll get. Where could we stop, though?" Mom replied.

"Head to J'Lambda," Juliet said.

"Are you sure? I doubt they'd accept us kindly."

"Maybe not, but they'll let us stay long enough to make the repairs."

"Alright, setting a course for J'Lambda."

"How far away is that?" I asked.

"Not terribly. It should take us five minutes from here," Mom replied.

I was shocked at how close we were stopping. Couldn't they catch up to us?

"Is it safe?"

"Yes, we won't be there for long at all. We'll be long gone before AL can even guess where we've headed," Mom reassured me.

"Alright, I trust you."

Leaning back in my chair, I finally managed to relax a little. The adrenaline in my body slowly began to dissipate, allowing me to feel the soreness in my arm where my father had gripped me. It was going to leave a bruise, no doubt, but as far as I could tell, nothing was broken. Unlike him, I managed to walk away without any broken bones. It made me smile, just thinking about what I did.

"Good job back there, dude. I saw what you did, badass," Nikki said, noticing how I was looking at my arm.

"It was pretty badass, wasn't it? I just punched a space tyrant in the face!"

"A space tyrant who was also your dad, but that's not important!"

We laughed together, one of those deep laughs that has you clutching at your stomach. It wasn't all that funny, but we were both so delirious from the stress that it seemed like the most ridiculous thing in the world. Meanwhile, Juliet turned to mom.

"M4, do you want to talk about what happened?" She asked.

"About what?"

"What happened after the Omega Quasar."

Hearing them silenced the two of us, and we leaned forward to listen.

"Is there something we need to talk about?"

"No, no, I-I just wanted to say that my opinion of you hasn't changed. I'm sad that it happened, and I don't blame you at all, so don't worry."

The mood changed so quickly I almost got whiplash. However, it was very kind of her to say that she'd probably been waiting since the trial. Mom didn't move her head, focusing on the vast expanse of space in front of her.

"Thank you," She replied, the tiniest hint of a tremble in her voice.

The planet J'Lambda appeared in front of us as mom slowed the ship down. It was massive, with massive tracks of land surrounded by oceans. The ratio of land to water was about 3:1, so it appeared dryer than Earth, but this was canceled out by its enormous size.

At a much slower speed, Mom approached the planet, breaching the atmosphere. Juliet instructed her on where to land as the surface grew closer and closer. Buildings became visible as we passed through the cloud layer, rising up into the sky. They were decorated with colorful paint and cloth with beautiful patterns. In the center of it all was a massive building that looked like a castle.

We lowered the ship down into a field just outside the castle walls. With us in place, mom activated the cloaking device.

"Alright, I know a guy who can fix our ship inside. M4 and I will head in while the two of you stay here and guard the ship, alright?" Juliet explained.

"Right!" Nikki and I replied.

They nodded at us and got out of their seats. Mom walked over to the door first, opening it then turning around to say goodbye.

"We'll be right back," She said before turning around and realizing the ship was surrounded by guards armed with blasters. "Never mind, we're all going now."

The guards swarmed the ship, driving all of us out. When they saw Juliet, they glared. They led us out with blasters aimed at our backs, leading us inside the castle through the front gate. From there, it was only a short walk to the throne room, a massive chamber filled with art, sculptures, and at the center, two thrones. Seated on them were a man and woman, both dark-skinned, wearing clothes similar to the ones I had worn at the announcement. At the sight of us all, they cringed.

Regal and proud, the man sat with his face forward with perfect posture. His wife was similar. They both seemed to emanate pure grace and dignity. Their presence made me feel small and insignificant in comparison. The woman's hair was long and beautiful, braided halfway down, then free-flowing to the ends with gold accessories holding the braids in place. Her hair was so beautiful, the kind of pretty that made you think it was fake, but it wasn't. The man had short hair neatly trimmed in the front with two protrusions that resembled a pair of Bantu knots or maybe a bun, I couldn't tell from this distance, on the side of his head.

The guards led us to the bottom of the steps leading up to the platform the thrones sat on. With us in place, they bowed and stepped back.

"Mother, Father, It's been a long time," Juliet said.

"You have a lot of nerve showing your face around here after what you did," The man spoke.

"And you," He added, pointing to my mother. "I should kill you where you stand for what you did. Corrupting my daughter, leading her in a war that wasn't even real, bringing disgrace to our family!"

Mom gulped, looking down.

"Father, listen to me, AL1TH1US lied to you. M4 was never a spy!" Juliet argued.

"Quiet! You've brought enough shame to our family. I'd have you killed if it weren't for the trouble it would cause."

"Sir, please, I implore you," Mom began. "We mean no trouble. Our ship is damaged, all we ask is enough time to make essential repairs, then we'll be far out of your hair."

"Why? Why should we help you after what you did?"

"If you help us, I'll be gone. You'll never have to worry about us again." Juliet proposed.

Her father thought it over for a moment, looking between the five of us.

"You will never be able to return, you understand?"

"I know, but the war I'm fighting is worth it." She replied.

"Alright. You have until your ship is fixed, then I expect you to leave my planet."

"Understood," Mom and Juliet replied, bowing.

"J0SHU4!" Juliet's mother called.

A young man wearing beautiful but minimalist clothing appeared in the door wearing an old looking leather aviator's cap with slightly yellowed goggles. When he saw Juliet, he threw his arms wide.

"Well, if it isn't the family's second-biggest disappointment?" He joked.

"Brother!" Juliet replied, accepting his hug.

Her parents just sat and watched with disgust, rolling their eyes at how nonchalant the two were acting.

"What brings you home, sis?"

"I'm-" Juliet began, but stopped, turning to her parents. "There are too many ears here, let's head outside and chat."

"Sure thing."

Juliet walked to the exit with her arm around her brother, the rest of us followed. This time the guards allowed us to pass. Before we'd made it out of the throne room, mom paused. I turned to see what was stopping her and found her turned to look back at Juliet's parents.

"I have to say. Your daughter was a model soldier. She was my most trusted ally both then, and now, you should be proud," She said, turning and leaving before they could reply.

"Damn sis, how'd you get your hands on this?" Josh exclaimed in awe at the sight of the Assayer.

"It's not mine. Belongs to Galileo."

"To who?"

"AL1TH1US's son." Juliet said, gesturing to me.

169

"Didn't know he had a son. Good for him, I guess," Josh said, admiring the side of the ship.

He winced at the sight of the holes the blaster had put in the hull, shaking his head.

"He announced it a few hours ago. Didn't you watch it?"

"No, I'm not much for politics, you know that sis."

He continued along the body of the ship, touching it occasionally in what looked like an educated sort of way, like a mechanic messing with a car.

"Can you fix it?" Mom asked.

"Absolutely. It's going to take me a minute to get up to speed with all the fancy new upgrades, but it won't take me more than a day."

"Is there anything we can get you to help?" Nikki asked, trying to be helpful.

"Nope, I'm good, stranger."

"Oh, sorry, my name's Nikki. I'm from Earth."

"Earth? That doesn't sound familiar." Josh said as he pulled his hat over his eyes.

From his pockets, he produced strange glowing tools, two in each hand, and set them aside. He picked up one and got to work, removing the black burn marks from the side.

"It's where M4 ended up when she was running away."

"Your terrorist friend?"

"I'm not a terrorist. Freedom fighter," Mom protested.

"You know I was wondering if that was you," Josh laughed.

"Enough about that, what about here? Who's next in line now?" Juliet asked.

"JUN1P3R, although it was gonna be me, but I absolutely refused."

"Here kids, let's go relax somewhere and let him work," Mom

said, pulling Nikki and me away.

She led us to a clearing nearby, leaving Joshua and Juliet to catch up. We found a patch of grass that seemed free of rocks and debris and took a seat. Nikki stretched out completely, putting her hands behind her head to settle in for a nap, unlike mom and I, who chose to sit up.

"Do you need to take a nap, ma? I can stay up and keep watch if you want," I offered.

"No, I'm fine, how about you?"

"I'm good. I was actually hoping we could talk a little."

"Oh, well, let me get comfy," Mom said, extending her arms behind her to rest on.

She gave me a nod to go on once she got in a position she found pleasing. I had a lot to ask, but one question burned on my mind the most.

"Why did you rebel exactly? What was the inciting incident?" I asked.

"It happened when I was still general. I had just gotten back from conquering a planet, although we didn't call it that we called it 'assimilating.' I was always told that when we invaded a world, we were doing it for them, that we'd bring science, culture, medicine, and all sorts of things life-changing with us. That was all I had ever known, I never saw the truth until one day I went to a small town on the outskirts of the city to have some repairs done on Starhopper. There was a woman there who I recognized as being from the planet I had recently conquered. She had a basket of fruit in her hands. She tripped as I was walking by, so I ran over to help, and when I did, she screamed and pushed me away. Then when I tried to check on her, she flinched like she was afraid of me. I didn't understand why she would be acting that way, it was like she saw me as a monster when really we were supposed to be equals, so I decided to look into it. I checked the records of that planet and found that 70 percent of them had been taken as slaves. The other 30 were either killed or managed to escape. It shocked me, so I looked into other planets we'd conquered and found the same thing."

"Do they turn every planet they conquer into slave labor?"

"No, it depends on what the planet has to offer and the state of the people on it. If the people are advanced enough, they were allowed to join society, but if they don't meet the standards set by AL1, their resources are stolen, and their people turned to slaves."

"That's terrible."

It was nice to know what part of the government mom disliked. She had always just said it was corrupt, but now I could tell she had a much more reasonable explanation for rebelling. If I were her, I'd have done the same.

"Why did you kill Rosalina's dad?" I asked.

That was another thing I wondered about. What could her reasoning be for killing an innocent man?

"Who?"

"Sorry that young girl that was with dad."

"Oh yes, L3L4ND. He was exactly what The Senate looked for in a soldier. He did exactly what he was told, never questioned anything, and took advantage of the power he had. I never liked him, out of all my commanding officers; he was my least favorite from the start, but that wasn't why I killed him. He had just had a child, a baby girl, with a woman who I learned, was from a planet we'd conquered. I was happy for him at first, but then the mother died unexpectedly. I went to console him and found he didn't even seem to be affected by her death. When

I asked him about it, he told me she was nothing to him, that he had seen her while we were conquering and took her for his own sick pleasure. The pregnancy was an accident, and he killed her as soon as the child was born."

"Oh my god."

"I know, so on the day I was to receive my medal of honor, I shot him to show the world I was loyal to The Rebellion. I wanted to terrify the higher-ups, so by killing my subordinate, I showed them I was a bigger threat than they could have imagined."

"I don't think dad ever told her about her mother. He probably kept it a secret from her."

"Makes sense. If he told her she would question things further and learn the truth."

Pausing for a moment, I worked through which question I wanted to ask next. Deciding, I shifted in place and spoke up.

"Why did they say you corrupted JUL?"

"That one's easy. You see, JUL was next in line to be queen of J'Lambda, and their society has a rule that before you can assume the throne, you must serve your people's military. I can't remember if you had to do it for a certain amount of time or earn some sort of accomplishment, either way, she became one of my commanders due to her status. We worked together for a long time and developed a level of trust that none of the other commanders had. She respected me, so when she caught me one night sneaking back into the barracks carrying a jacket with rebel markings, she was conflicted. I explained my reasoning behind why I joined and what I was fighting for, which was convincing enough for her. The next day instead of reporting me, she asked me to take her with me."

"Were you and dad really engaged?"

Mom sighed, looking off into the distance.

"Yes. I used to be in love with him. I wanted to marry him and start a family, but then I learned about what he was doing. When I confronted him about what he was doing to planets and people, he said he couldn't change it, that it was out of his hands, and at that moment, I lost all respect for him."

"I'm so sorry, mom."

"Don't be, you have nothing to be sorry for," She said, gently placing her hand on mine.

"It's got to hurt just seeing me. I remind you of him, don't I, and that's got to hurt."

Mom made a face, a mix between sad and worried. She pursed her lips and exhaled.

"Galileo, do you know why I named you that?"

"No."

"The night I came to Earth, remember I said I panicked and hid in what would become our house."

"Yeah."

"Well, once the rain had stopped, I went exploring. On the second floor, in what is now your bedroom, was a long cylindrical object facing the window and pointed up. I didn't know what it was, so I looked through the little piece on the end and noticed the stars seemed so much closer. Not knowing where I was, I was overjoyed when I realized this object could help me orient myself, so I tried to use it to find my home. Earth was so far out of my known universe, however, that I didn't recognize anything, but it did bring me comfort to know that if I didn't know where I was, there was a good chance The Senate wouldn't either. On the side of that object, in gold lettering, was the word Galileo, which I thought was its name. It wasn't till after you were born that I learned it was actually called a telescope."

"I was named after a telescope?"

"That's not the point. The point is, I named you in a way that was unlike how The Senate chooses to define people because I wanted you to be more than that. I gave you a name that would let you define who you were, not who your parents were or where you were born, based on something that brought me comfort. You are removed from The Senate, its beliefs, and your father."

"That's lovely, mom."

"You're welcome, telescope."

14

Chapter 14

To fix the holes in the Assayer, Joshua had to get scrap metal from his collection. He walked past me, mom, and Nikki with his arms full of random shiny pieces. It looked heavy, but when we offered to help, he denied.

He took them over to the side of the ship and set them down by his tools. As he needed them, he picked them up. Nikki was still asleep, but the noise from his repairs woke her up.

"What's that noise?"

"Josh is doing the last of the repairs now," I replied.

"Oh that sounds cool, let's go watch," She suggested, standing up and walking over that way.

I looked over at mom to see what she thought, with her nod of approval, we got up and headed that way.

The ship looked terrific. The only sign of anything happening to it were the holes on the side, and he was working on those. The ugly burn marks were gone, without a hint of tarnish. There was no warping to the shape either, it was as smooth as it had been the day dad gave it to me.

"Dude, that's incredible!" I exclaimed, running over to get a closer look.

"Thanks, can't say it was easy," Josh replied, grabbing a piece of scrap metal.

"Where'd you learn to do all this?" Nikki asked.

"I taught myself."

"No way! I don't believe that."

"Well, believe it, little lady, I did it all by myself. My parents didn't want me to be an engineer, but I couldn't help myself. It was too fun tinkering with things."

"Can I watch you do the last part?" Nikki begged.

"Sure, but you've gotta wear these otherwise, it'll damage your eyes," He replied, tossing her a dark pair of goggles.

As she put hers on, he hit a button on his aviator hat that turned his goggles from yellow to black. Once she had hers in place, they flashed blue, letting us all know that they were active. The rest of us looked away and allowed him to get to work welding.

It didn't take him too long, but by the time he was approaching being finished, the sun was starting to set. He had one more hole left, a small one near the front, but he didn't have any more scrap metal sitting in his pile. He scratched his head at the sight, hitting the button to change his goggles back so he could get a better look.

"I thought I grabbed enough. Hey, Galileo, can you go check and see if I dropped a piece on the way here?" He asked.

"Sure thing," I replied, heading that way.

I passed mom and Juliet, who were lying down in the grass, looking up at the sky. They were talking about something, but I didn't catch any of it.

My first instinct was to look over by where we had all been sitting earlier. Although I didn't remember hearing anything drop, we were chatting, so it was possible I just didn't hear it over what we were saying.

There wasn't anything in the clearing, so I moved to start looking in the direction he'd come from out of the woods. The trees weren't overly dense, so it was easy for me to maneuver around.

"Looking for something, son?" A voice came from over to my right.

I whipped around in fear, hoping I was mistaken, but the sight of my father sitting on a log with the piece of scrap metal in his hand proved my suspicions. He was just sitting there, by himself, legs crossed. I couldn't tell if he had a weapon on him, but that didn't matter, he could have soldiers surrounding us.

"Your nose looks better," I said, harking back to our most recent encounter.

"Yes, it feels better too. Nothing the nanites couldn't fix."

"How'd you find us?"

"You remember I told you your ship had the finest equipment possible? The finest safety features, engine, and tracking devices," He explained, turning the metal in his hands.

How could I have forgotten something so important? Of course, he would have put a tracker on the ship.

"So, what's your plan? Going to drag us all back, lock us up? Listen, I'll go with you. I don't care just let mom and Nikki go. I'll do whatever you say just don't hurt them," I pleaded.

Dad stood up, walking towards me with a blank expression on his face. He was impossible to read, which scared me to no end. Just a few feet away from me, he stopped, tapping the metal against his hand.

"No, I came to ask you something."

"What?"

"I've been doing a lot of thinking, about you, your mother, The Rebellion, our society as a whole. Tell me, son, are you doing this because it's what your mother suggests or because it's what you want to do?" He asked.

He made me realize I hadn't thought about it before. I had been following mom up until this point, doing whatever she suggested because that's all I've ever known in regards to space, but yesterday when she told me why I began forming my own opinion. It wasn't about mom and dad anymore, but the big picture and the people whose lives were affected.

"I'm doing it for me. Mom told me about how you enslave people, that's not right. A civilized society shouldn't do that!" I replied boldly.

"I know."

"You should be- wait what?"

"I know. I agree with your mother, it's not right, but there's nothing I can do about it."

"You're the king, aren't you?"

"Yes, but it's not that simple! Can you imagine what would happen if I were to tell everyone to change their lives completely? If I told them their way of life, the only thing they've ever known was wrong there'd be chaos. Even if it didn't directly impact them, they'd still panic at the prospect of change. I tried explaining that to your mother, but she wouldn't listen."

He made a valid point. People don't like it when their government tries to change their lifestyle, we've seen that before. To completely change people's perspectives would take time, it couldn't all be done at once.

"I see."

"If you're doing this because you want to, then I'm not going to stop you. If Earth is where you'd rather be, then that's fine, but I need to know that it is what you want," He said, placing a hand on my shoulder.

"It is."

He gave me a crooked smile, placing the scrap metal in my hand. His hand lingered there for a moment as he looked me in the eyes.

"I love you, son. Please don't hate me."

"I don't."

He pulled me forward and gave me a hug. When we separated, he let go and turned away. Without looking back, he walked off into the woods, probably back to whatever ship he had taken to get here.

When I returned with the metal, everyone wanted to know what took me so long. Not wanting them to know what happened, I made up an excuse on the spot.

"Sorry, took me forever to find this thing."

"That's alright. Hand it over, and I'll finish this up so you guys can get out of here," Josh said, holding his hand out.

Once the last hole was patched, the ship looked good as new. I don't know what kind of mad science he'd used, but it didn't even look like he'd done any welding. It was impossible to tell where the holes had been, and the thruster looked identical to all the others.

"Incredible as always, brother," Juliet complemented.

"Thanks, sis. You really should come visit more often. I miss ya sometimes," Josh replied.

"If only I felt the same," Juliet joked, earning her a punch on the shoulder.

"Good luck, you guys. I'm rooting for you."

"Thanks again for everything," Mom said, bowing to him.

"Don't worry about it. I had a good time."

Mom walked over and touched the side panel, opening the door to step inside. Turning around, she waved to Josh then headed further inside. Juliet followed suit, waving similarly before walking off.

"Thanks for letting me watch you. That was really cool," Nikki said.

"No problem, I'm always happy to show off for whoever will watch. See ya, Earthling."

"See ya."

Nikki joined the others inside the ship, leaving me to say goodbye.

"Thanks for fixing my ship. You did a great job."

"All this flattery is gonna make me sick," He laughed.

"I hope we get to see you again someday," I said, hopping on board.

When the ship started, it sounded good as new. There were no more warning signs this time, so we could sit and enjoy the ride in peace. With all of us in our seats, mom slowly raised the ship off the ground, it moved as smooth silk.

From his place on the ground, Josh waved goodbye with both hands. It was sweet to see him wishing us luck, it made me feel a little more at ease. Once we'd cleared the treeline, mom switched it into high gear and took off towards Earth, throwing us back against our seats.

I was right about how much of a pain things were going to be when we got home. Hiding the spaceship was no problem thanks to its cloaking device, but hiding the fact that we'd been gone for so long was another story.

Mom had to explain to her boss why she left out of the blue and didn't come back. She made up some story about how she'd been falsely arrested. Surprisingly he bought it, or he just didn't want to go through the trouble of finding another loyal employee like mom. If I had to bet, I'd say it was the latter.

Nikki's parents didn't notice she'd been missing since they hadn't come home yet, but her babysitter was pissed. Then she had to explain to the school where she'd been. While I went with the more sensible option of claiming a family emergency, Nikki went the grand route. She tried to say she was in the hospital with appendicitis. It was funny watching her explain the pain to her teachers.

Juliet moved in with mom and me until we could figure out what our next move was. She was a great houseguest too, always helping with cleaning, cooking, never making a sound, it was fantastic. It was charming getting to see mom with a friend around, she was so happy.

Everything seemed to be back to normal, although we made sure to scan for invaders at least three times a day.

About a week after we got back, I was relaxing on the couch when I heard a knock at the door. Mom had sent Juliet to the store with some money, one of her new chores, so I assumed it was her returning. I got up and opened the door without checking the peephole.

I was not at all expecting to see my dad standing there.

"Is your mother home?" My father said.

I slammed the door in his face before he could say anymore, my heart racing. Mom heard the commotion and came to see what was going on.

"Who is it?" She asked, opening the door.

When she saw my father, she did the same thing I did. He tried knocking again, but we ignored him.

"Don't worry, I just want to have a word with you two," He

said from outside.

"Yeah, right! I don't trust a word you have to say," Mom replied.

"Well, I'm not going to leave until you hear me out," He said, his voice muffled by the door.

"I think he's serious, mom."

"I know he is."

Mom looked around the room, rubbing her chin to think. She tapped her foot in thought before groaning. When she opened the door, he was still standing in the same spot.

"What do you want?" She asked with venom in her words.

"I think the two of you will want to see this," He replied, pulling out his holopad.

There was a video on the screen, and when he clicked it, it began to play. In the video, we could see him standing at the same podium where he announced my existence. From the looks of it, there were just as many people there as there had been then.

"This may come as a shock to many of you, but after talking with M4, I have decided to begin an era of societal reformation to accommodate members of the former rebellion. We discussed and found that while The Rebellion had many ideas that were far too extreme, they still exposed major flaws in our society; ones that I believe need to be addressed. I will be working with The Senate to make this transition as smooth as possible, so you all do not need to worry. For now, just do things as you always would, and let us fix the problem."

We heard the crowd start muttering before he put the video away. It was a mix of confusion and disapproval, but at least they weren't yelling.

"That was two days ago. The senators are already screaming

at me to explain myself, but I'm not ready yet," He said.

"Why not?" Mom asked.

"Because I want the two of you there with me. I want you to help me with this," He explained.

"Why's that?" I questioned.

"M4, you know The Rebellion's wishes better than anyone; no one else could be better suited for this job. And Galileo, I want you to be there so you can learn from it. You're going to be king after me, so it would be a good chance for you to learn, but more than that, I want my family with me," Dad said, getting down on his knees.

It was weird seeing him like that. He grabbed mom's hand as he awaited her response.

"I can never forgive you for what you did," She said.

"I don't expect you to."

"I will always remember, you won't be able to make me forget."

"I would never try to, but do you think, for the sake of what you believe, you could put all that aside and work with me?" Dad asked, looking up at her expectantly.

Mom took a deep breath and sighed. She closed her eyes and thought about it for a moment.

"Alright, I'll work with you, not because I forgive you, but for those who stand for the cause and those who would benefit."

"Thank you," Dad replied with a bow.

"I'll go too, but it's going to have to wait a little. School isn't over yet, so I can't leave," I piped up.

"Wonderful. M4, if you'll start packing, we'll leave as soon as possible, then Galileo can join us when he's ready. May I come in?"

"Sure, just don't wander around too much," Mom commanded, heading to her room to get started.

Dad took a few steps in, and I led him over to the couch, offering him a seat. He sat down slowly, like he was testing it out. Once he was seated, he wiggled around to further test it out.

"Comfy," He laughed.

I sat down next to him and put my feet up on the coffee table, pulling out my phone to tell Nikki the excellent news.

"Guess who's going back to space?" I sent.

"You and me." She replied.

"What makes you think you're invited?"

"What makes you think I need to be invited?"

"Touche."

"That's right. Rendezvous tonight for further reconnaissance, I'll bring provisions this time."

"Roger that."

We must have forgotten to close the door all the way because Juliet stepped inside without having to knock or fiddle with the lock.

"I'm back, everyone, they were all out of-" She stopped when she saw dad sitting on the couch.

"Hello," He said.

"What the hell?!" She yelled, dropping the groceries.

Note

Any instances of a name where it is written as a combination of letters and numbers should be read as a serial number.

For example,

M4T1LD4 should be read M Four T One L D Four.

R0 should be read R Zero